ENTWINED WITH HIM

The Merge Series, Book 3

KYLIE KENT

McCartney Industries Pty Ltd.

Ebook ISBN 13: 978-0-6489981-4-3
Paperback ISBN 13: 978-0-6489981-5-0

Cover Illustration by
RJ CREATIVES GRAPHIC SERVICES

Editing services provided by
Kat Pagan - https://www.facebook.com/PaganProofreading

Trigger Warnings

This book contains scenes and discussions of self-harm, profanity, sexual content and violence. If any of these are triggers for you, you should consider skipping this read.

Please Stalk Me

Come and check out my website and join my mailing list to stay up to date and gain access to bonus materials.
Website & Newsletter: https://www.kyliekent.com/

If you want early access to everything, yes everything come and join my Patreon Group Kylie Kent Patreon

Want to be involved in discussions and have access to tons of give-aways? Join my readers group on Facebook Kylie's Steam Room

Facebook: @kyliekent2020
Instagram Follow: @author_kylie_kent_

Dedication

Dedicated to my friend Catharina. Cat, I couldn't choose a better person to be growing and developing alongside during my writing journey. Throughout the development of Entwined, you have taught me a great deal of knowledge. You have encouraged me to be the best version of myself that I can be; for that, I will be forever grateful to you and for you.

Blurb

Ella

It's been four years since I picked myself up off the floor and made a plan to escape. Sometimes, the grass is not greener on the other side; it's darker.

University was my fresh start.

A life away from him.

It wasn't enough. I couldn't escape the memories.

My demons are not ones you can see. No, they're well hidden. They stay in the dark, haunting every second of my being. I fight every day to be better, to not give in.

I'm back now.

I'm better now.

I can handle being back here in the club.

I can handle being around him again.

At least, that's what I thought. All my well laid plans go up in flames when my eyes land on him.

Dean, my brother's best friend.

Dean, the one man I've always loved.

Dean

Four years ago, I did the hardest thing I've ever had to do.

I walked away from the love of my life.

She was young; she needed to go and live her dreams, without me dragging her into my darkness.

She's also the little sister of my best friend.

Now, Ella is back, and she's not eighteen anymore.

I'm not going to make the same mistake twice.

She is mine. I will make sure everyone knows it, including her.

She claims she's broken. Broken or not, she is my one.

Always has been. Always will be.

Entwined

ENTWINED

'WIND OR TWIST TOGETHER, INTERWEAVE.'

Prologue

Ella

FOUR YEARS earlier

"OH MY GOD, Ella, there is no way your brothers are letting you in the club wearing that dress," Niki says as we make our way down the street.

"Maybe not, but neither of them will let me walk back out the doors in this dress either, so the way I see it, they have to let me stay in there." I run my hands down my short—very short—black dress. It's skin tight, showing off my tiny waist and sizeable rear end. For a moment, I question my choice of outfit. I don't usually wear dresses this short, but tonight, I wanted to stand out. I wanted him to finally notice me as a woman, and not as his best friend's little sister.

We're heading to my brother's club; Zac owns The Merge. It's currently Sydney's number one club, the place everyone wants to be. The line at the door is already leading down the street. I take Niki's hand and drag her to the front of the line, despite the dirty looks of all the people who have been waiting.

They can hate me all they like, but the one benefit of being the little sister is skipping the queue. As I get to the rope at the front of the entrance, the bouncer's eyes go wide. He immediately says something into his earpiece, more than likely letting Dean, his boss, my brother's best friend and head of security—oh, and also the one guy I want and can't have—know that I arrived.

Good, let him come down here and see what he's missing out on. An evil smile crosses my face; this is the reason for this dress. I want Dean to be out of his mind, to see that I'm not just a little girl anymore.

"So, was it Dean or Zac you were so quick to dob me into?" I ask as I stop in front of the bouncer.

He looks unsettled, unsure what to say or do. He finally says, "Sorry, Ella. I have strict instructions to let Dean know whenever you walk through these doors. You need to go straight up to the VIP section." The bouncer, who seems to know my name yet I have no clue who he is, holds the door open for us.

Walking into The Merge is an experience in and of itself. Although I've been here plenty of times during the day, while Zac was working, I'd either spend my afternoons sitting in his office doing home-work or down in the basement watching Bray train.

Zac, my oldest brother, has been my guardian since I was thirteen when our parents died. He has been the best, considering he was only twenty at the time. He always puts my needs first, never missed a school event. I will be forever grateful to Zac for the way he stepped up and took care of Bray and me.

Bray, the middle child in the family, is the typical middle child. He struggled the most when our parents died; he got into a lot of trouble as a teenager, which Zac always managed to drag him out of. Don't get me wrong, he's a great brother; he would do anything for me. Although they can be overbearing most of the time, I wouldn't trade my brothers for anyone. I also would never admit that to them.

The Merge is packed already; it's only ten o'clock and there are people lining the deep red walls of the club. Zac really did a great job building this place. The small intimate sections scattered across the lower floor are all filled with people. Zac had all the tables designed to represent couples in the throes of passion, his vision of bodies merging together.

When I was younger, I was never allowed on this floor; he used to take me in through the back, up the lift and straight to his office. It wasn't until I was sixteen that I finally saw what all the fuss was about. Let's just say, these sculptures made my little sixteen-year-old brain blush the first time I saw them.

Now that I'm eighteen, I don't blush so much anymore; but as I look at the sculptures I'm walking by on the way to the VIP section, I picture what it would feel like to have Dean's body wrapped around mine in these positions.

It's never going to happen though. It's a far-off pipe dream. Dean is loyal to Zac, ten years my senior and only sees me as his best friend's little sister. Hopefully this little black dress tonight is going to change his view of me.

Niki and I are already on our third cosmopolitan. I'm feeling the beginning of a buzz coming on. I'm also feeling the very urgent need to pee. I lean over the table to yell out over the music to tell her that I'm heading to the bathroom.

"I'll be back. Nature's calling." I point in the direction of the bathroom.

"Want me to come with?"

I shake my head; there's no need to take her with me. I have no doubt that there are at least two of Dean's security guys hiding in the shadows somewhere, watching my every move.

As I stand and make my way through the crowd to the bathroom, I stumble slightly—it's the heels. I haven't drunk that much yet. That's what I'm telling myself anyway.

The best thing about the VIP floor: there's no queues at the bathroom. When I enter the ladies' room, it's empty, quiet—the loud noise of the club muted behind these doors. I hear the door open and shut while I'm in the cubicle. Finishing up, I open the cubicle door and head over to the sinks.

Before I make it there, I'm grabbed from behind. A large hand comes around, covering my mouth. I'm momentarily stunned and I freeze. I look up into the mirror and see a large guy with a sneer on his face, his eyes dark and sinister looking.

I remember every move Bray ever taught me and start to fight my way out of his hold. I bring my foot down on his and try to twist and turn, while landing punches anywhere I can.

"Fucking little bitch, you think you can fight me off? Go ahead, give me everything you got. It's just going to make me taking you all the sweeter." His hands start grabbing at my body; he roughly grabs my breast in one of his hands and proceeds to push me up against the wall.

I'm trapped, my front pressed against the wall with this fucker pressed against my back. I can feel his hardness digging into my back. I fight the urge to throw up. I just need to fight back. I will not lose my virginity to rape. But even as I'm thinking this, I know

5

I'm screwed. I can't fight off a guy this big. But I will not go down without a fight either.

I bring my leg up behind him and manage to connect my heel with his balls, not hard enough though. He grunts as he spins me around and punches me in the face. My vision goes blurry. I feel my body slump to the ground.

"Fucking slut, you'll pay for that. I'm going to slam my cock so hard into your little pussy, and when I'm done with that, I'll take your ass too."

One of his meaty hands holds me up by my upper arm as he backhands me across the face. I scream as loud as I can, even though I know it's hopeless. No one is going to hear me. One thing I do know for sure is that when Zac and Bray do find me, this guy won't be left breathing. That brings a smile to my face.

"You like it, you dirty little slut. I knew you would fucking love it." He smiles like he has won.

"You're fucking delusional. The only reason I'm smiling right now is because I know when my brothers find you, you're a dead man."

"Fuck you! Think your brothers scare me, bitch?"

The smile is wiped off my face as he punches me in the stomach. I fall to the floor, the pain radiating through my body. My brain wants to shut down; it wants to black out. I'm fighting to stay alert. I see a boot coming for my head. I brace myself for the hit I know is coming. My eyes squeeze closed and I hunch over, trying to protect my head the best I can.

I freeze in this position, waiting, except the kick

never comes. I hear loud shouts and shuffling. When I open my eyes again, Dean is leaning down over me. He's talking but I don't hear what he's saying.

I manage to pick myself up and crawl onto him. I bury my head in his chest and cling to his shirt. This is when I finally let myself cry. I finally feel like I can relax with the knowledge that I'm safe now.

"It's okay, El. I've got you," Dean says as he hugs me back just as tightly, his hand running through my hair, as he holds my head against his chest. I feel my body lift as he picks me up.

"Take the fucker down to the basement. I'm going to fucking kill him," Dean instructs the security guys who are currently picking up the unconscious asshole who attacked me.

Zac carries me from the car up to our apartment. I let him think I'm asleep, because, right now, in my brother's arms, I know nothing can get to me. I know no one can touch me. As safe as Zac makes me feel, it has nothing on the way I felt when I was in Dean's arms.

Dean's energy, the possessive protectiveness he was

radiating over me tonight, was like nothing I've ever felt or experienced. The promises he whispered into my ear, the ones no one else could hear, those are the words I'm trying to hold onto right now. Those are the words that bring me comfort.

When Zac carries me into the apartment, and I hear Dean tell him that he'll take me, I want to jump from my brother's arms and into Dean's. I don't though. I let them think that I'm asleep.

When I feel myself being passed over, I know it's Dean who I'm being passed to. His citrus scent assaults my senses. His tight hold of me as he walks down the hall warms me. My fist clenches around his shirt; there is no way I'm letting him let go of me.

Dean walks through my room, placing me on the bed. I hold on tight to his shirt; he's not leaving me here. He can't leave me here. I can't be in here by myself.

"Wait, don't leave me, please. Don't leave me here," I beg. I can feel myself start to panic.

"I'm not leaving you, Ella, just let me turn off the light and shut the door," he whispers.

"No, leave the light on, please."

"Okay, Princess, the light stays on." He untangles my hands from his shirt and makes his way over to the door, shutting it. I watch his every step, ready to jump up and follow him if he walks out.

He doesn't. He walks back over to the bed, takes his shoes off and lies down next to me. I then find myself wrapped in his arms, a place I never want to leave. This is how I cry myself to sleep, in his arms, with him whispering words of comfort in my ear.

Dean

I'll never be able to forget the image of her lying on the bathroom floor, bloodied and bruised. Most days, I wish I could bring the fucker who did that to her back to life, just to see the life strangled out of him again. I'd never been so fucking terrified of losing someone as I was when I saw her.

The emotions that ran through me scared the hell out of me. I'd always been protective of her, always wanted to shelter her from the world, from our world —the one her brothers and I were involved with. And ever since she turned sixteen, that need to protect her changed from me wanting to protect a little sister, to me wanting to protect the one whom I loved most in the world.

There was just one problem though, no matter how much I loved her, how much I wanted her, I knew I could never have her. Ella was my best friend's little sister—ten years younger than me.

The moment she turned eighteen, I struggled on a daily basis; she wasn't underage anymore. I didn't feel like such a creep, wanting someone who was under-age. She was legal and turning heads in any room she walked into.

She made no secret of how much she wanted me either, made no attempt to hide her feelings from me. The nights after her attack, she would call me in tears,

11

begging me to come and help her. I could never say no. It was risky, spending those nights in her room with her brother, my best friend, just down the hall.

But I couldn't deny her the comfort she was seeking. I couldn't hear her cry and not be the one to wipe those tears away. For two months, I spent those nights in her bed, whispering promises into her ear as she would cry herself to sleep.

I always snuck out in the mornings, before she would wake. I'd go home and jerk off in the shower, relieving the hard-on I'd suffer with all night long having her soft body in my arms—her scent surrounding me, torturing me all fucking night, and reminding me of what I couldn't have.

I knew I had to put a stop to the sleepovers when she started to want more from me than what I could give her. She was young. She needed to experience life, to have the full university experience without me dragging her down with my shit. She needed to be young and carefree, and if I claimed her like she wanted me to, like I fucking wanted to, she wouldn't be able to have that.

I entered her room one night. She was sitting on her bed, knees pulled up to her chest. She looked up at me as I approached the bed.

"Am I that broken that you can't imagine yourself being with me?" she asked, tears running down her face.

My steps faltered momentarily before I climbed on the bed and pulled her into my arms. "There is not a single thing broken about you, Ella. You are fucking perfect," I told her as I swiped at her tears with my thumb.

"Then why don't you want me?"

"We can't do this, Ella. You know I can't do this. I want you more than I've ever wanted anyone. But you're too young; you need to live your life. You need to be young." I wasn't strong enough to keep doing this. I needed to stop coming into her room. This would be the last time.

"I don't need to be young. I need you, Dean. I love you. I want you," she cried.

Fuck, everything in me wanted to give in, every fibre of my being wanted to claim her and make her mine. I didn't though. I kissed her gently, briefly, way too briefly.

"Ella, don't ever doubt that I fucking love you. I love you enough to let you go and live your life. I love you enough to put your needs above mine. I want you to have the life you're meant to have. I want you to go to university and be free. Be free of any troubles and worries. Not to be dragged down by being with me."

I stood up and walked out of her room. I left her falling apart on her bed. For the first time, since I can remember, I fucking cried. I went down to my car and fucking cried. I promised that one day, when the time was right, I would claim Ella as mine, despite knowing that Zac would want to kill me.

. . .

THAT WAS FOUR YEARS AGO; now she's coming back. She ended up transferring universities to Melbourne. I have only seen her on the rare occasions she has visited her brothers. She wouldn't talk to me; she would go out of her way to avoid being anywhere near me. But she's back now, and she will be mine.

Chapter One

Ella

WALKING INTO THE PENTHOUSE, I look around. Everything looks the same as it did when I left four years ago. It's not the same though. I drop my bag on the hall table on my way into the living room.

The same black leather U-shaped lounge, covered in navy and white cushions, fills the room. The view of Sydney Harbour greets me through the floor-to-ceiling windows, the sun shining high over the top of the Harbour Bridge.

It's weird being back here after spending the last four years avoiding the place — avoiding the memories — the good and the bad. The day after what I refer to in my mind as *the incident*, I applied for entry into Melbourne University. I knew I wouldn't be able to stay around here and be okay.

Making my way down the hall, I open my

bedroom door. I have not been back in here since the morning after the incident, when I picked myself up off my bedroom floor. I may have been able to pick up my body off the floor, but my heart, my soul, is still left in pieces.

I can see it like it was yesterday, the incident: me begging Dean to stay, not to leave me, then watching him walk out the door without so much as a backward glance. He chose to walk away, taking a piece of me with him, leaving me broken inside.

I haven't slept in this room since that night. I packed a bag and went to stay at Bray's house until it was time for me to make the move to Melbourne. Let's just say that conversation did not go over well with my brother Zac; he attempted to demand that I stay in Sydney.

It was a fight I was not backing down from though, and in the end, I won. It helped that Bray, when he finally woke up from the coma, was on my side. Oh yeah, my brother was shot by some crazy dude at The Merge. He ended up in a coma for two months. I honestly thought he would never wake up. He did though, and when he saw Zac and me arguing about me moving to Melbourne one day in his hospital room, he took pity on me. He told Zac to let me go, that it would be good for me.

He knew; Bray was the only person I ever told about my feelings for Dean. He also knew how heartbroken I was over the whole Dean not wanting me back scenario. Although he fought for me to be able to move to Melbourne, as soon as he was able to, he was on a flight once a month to check up on me.

Zac made fortnightly trips for the first six months. Then Alyssa gave birth to my ever-adorable nephew, Ash. Zac's visits became monthly after that, always bringing Alyssa and Ash with him. The thought of Ash made me smile; the one good thing about being back is I'm going to get to spend so much time being Aunty Ella to him and my twin nieces.

Fate has a funny way of coming back at you. Reilly, Bray's wife gave him two girls, twin girls, who I often remind him are going to be teenagers before he knows it. Lily and Hope are only one and a half now —the cutest little red-headed, green-eyed little girls. Thankfully they take after their mother, Reilly, Bray's wife.

Zac and Bray are both living out the dream, happily married with children and families of their own. As much as they include me in everything they do, and I do mean every little thing, it's not the same. I want the kind of love they have with their wives. I want someone to love me as fiercely as Zac loves Alyssa. I want someone to fight for me, the way Bray fights for Reilly.

I'm not sure that's ever going to be in my future. I'm too broken. I'm tainted by scars both inside and out. You would only see them if you got close enough, and I don't allow anyone that close. The only person who has seen all my scars, really seen them, is Bray.

And that's only because he caught me at one of my lowest moments.

Two years ago, Bray came down for one of his surprise visits. Bray, being Bray, let himself in. Me being me, I was totally oblivious that he was there, my bathroom door open, razor in hand, and eyes closed as the razor broke through the skin. Euphoria erupted throughout my body; peace overcame my hectic mind as I was engulfed by the bliss of the pain.

Bray was beside himself. After sitting down—me crying and him holding me in a vice grip as if he was worried that I was going to fly away—he finally calmed down a little. He stayed in my apartment for the next two weeks, researched therapists, and went with me to sessions with five different therapists until I found one whom I was comfortable with.

During those two weeks, Bray also made me join a gym and take up boxing classes. His rationale was some crap about exercise making people happy. I didn't correct him that I wasn't unhappy per se, just broken.

I didn't cut because I was sad. I cut because I needed the pain. The pain not only made me feel alive, it became a distraction to the thoughts inside my head. It was like a drug, and I was addicted to the high that I got from it. I was addicted to the escape it offered.

Bray was right though; exercise did make me feel more balanced. I didn't stop cutting, but I can now go a few months at a time without cutting. I didn't need it as much as I used to. I kept up my weekly therapy sessions. Bray made me promise; he said he wouldn't tell anyone if I kept up with the therapy.

Thinking about cutting now, especially being in this room, is bringing on the urge to do just that. I can feel my skin itching, feel my heart pick up.

Shaking thoughts of the past from my head, I walk out of my room, shut the door behind me and head to Bray's room. I can't be in that bedroom. Dropping my bag on Bray's bed, I dig through until I find my workout clothes. I need to hit the gym before I give in to the urge coursing through me.

I spend the next hour running on the treadmill. I have "Fight Song" by Rachel Platten blasting from the speakers. I jump off the treadmill, my mind set on the punching bag. I really want to hit something right now. I turn around and come to a stop, my hand coming up to my heart.

"Jesus Christ, Bray, give a girl a warning next time you're going to creep up," I yell at him over the music.

Bray laughs, walks over to the wall and turns the music down.

"First, not creeping; you should be more aware of your surroundings, Sis. Second, come here and give your favourite brother a hug."

"I'm all sweaty, Bray. You don't want to hug me right now." I start to walk towards the bag hanging from the rafters — I still want to hit something. Before I reach the bag, I'm picked up and spun around.

"Damn it, Bray, put me down!" I try to get a punch in, but with the way he's holding me, my fists are only greeted by air. By the time he puts me back on my feet, I'm dizzy and stumble back a step.

As soon as I get my bearings, I punch his arm. "Don't mess with me, asshole. I'm not in the mood," my voice growls at him.

"Aww, little Ella wants to take on the champ? Okay, bring it. Give me all you got, little girl."

Bray starts jumping around with his fists up; little does he know I've gotten good at this. Right now, I also have enough built-up anger and frustration that I need to expel somewhere. Why not direct that at the pretty boy's face?

Smiling at him, I laugh a little before swinging and landing a right hook on his jaw. His head swings to the side. I caught him off guard. I wait for him to pounce on me but he doesn't. He just looks at me with a dumbfounded expression on his face.

"Damn, Ella, where the hell did you learn to punch like that?" he asks.

Shrugging my shoulders, I hold my hands up,

ready to strike again. "I've been practicing. Come on, there's more where that came from."

"Uh-huh, I'm sure. First though, how long?" he questions.

Every time I talk to him, he will ask me the same question: *how long?* How long has it been since I have cut? I always answer honestly. I can't lie to him; he'd probably be able to tell anyway.

"Six months," I say with a smile, because three months is the longest time I've gone before that.

"Good, let's keep that number growing. Put your arms down before you hurt yourself. I'm not fighting you, Sweetheart."

As he goes to walk away, I stick my foot out, tripping him. I pounce on his back as he's falling to the ground and cling on to him like a monkey.

"Aww, is Brayden Williamson scared of his little sister? What will the fans think?" I tease.

Bray hasn't fought since he got shot. He had to retire from the cage. He now owns and runs a chain of MMA gyms he calls Club M. The original Club M —the fight club they used to run out of the basement of Zac's club, the one they thought I didn't know about—well, the boys closed it down. Everything Zac and Bray do now is way above board.

"Brat, get off me!" Bray turns over, dropping me on the floor and pinning me down. He looks down at me; it's like he can see into my damn soul when he stares like that.

He tilts his head before standing up and reaching

his hand down to help me. He doesn't let go after I'm standing. Instead, he wraps his arm around my shoulder and walks us towards the door.

"How are you going to be, seeing him every day again?" Bray squeezes my shoulder.

He's referring to Dean. I'm going to be taking over a lot for Zac at the club. "I don't know," I answer honestly.

"Well, you call me. If you can't handle it, call me."

I nod my head in response. Honestly, I'm scared as hell over how I'm going to cope. Seeing him every day… What if he has a girlfriend? Or if he just has girls all over him all the time? I don't know if I can handle that. It's been four years. I should be over him. I should have moved on years ago. I'm not though, and I never moved on—still secretly wanting him, waiting for him.

Chapter Two

Dean

SHE'S GOING to be here today. Ella. She won't be able to ignore me anymore. I'm going to make fucking sure of it. I've just sat in Zac's office with him, going over the increased security plans he wants in place now that Ella will be working here. Like I'd let anything fucking happen to her anyway.

Walking into the control room, I notice that every fucker is standing around the wall of screens, their attention on one screen in particular. What the fuck are they looking at?

"A hundred bucks says he closes!" Sam shouts.

"Nah, that chick's way out of even *his* league." Lachlan shakes his head.

Curiosity piqued, I walk over to see what the fuck they're carrying on about. When I see who is on the screen, my blood boils.

"Not a fucking chance. Any of you fuckers even think about touching her, I'll fucking kill you. That's if her brothers don't get to you first," I yell at them as I storm out of the room, heading straight for the first floor.

By the time I get to where she is, that fucker Shawn has his grubby paws on her, touching her arm as he says something in her ear. Ella's eyes go wide as she sees me storming up behind him. I grab his shirt and pull him off her. I don't even think as I uppercut him in the gut. He hunches over, before falling to the ground. *Fucker.* I want to fucking kill him.

I'm about to jump on him, to finish him off, when her voice breaks through my haze of rage.

"What the fuck, Dean?" Ella shoves past me to head towards Shawn, like she's going to help the fucker up.

Not a fucking chance. Wrapping an arm around her waist, I pick her up and spin her around. Standing so that I'm blocking her view of the whiny bastard on the floor while leaning in, I growl in her ear, "If you so much as touch him, Princess, I will fucking kill him — *that's a promise.*"

Ella's eyes go wide in shock before she composes herself, crossing her arms over her chest, which only draws my attention to her breasts — her black button-up sheer blouse doing nothing to hide the black bra underneath. Jesus Christ, I can see I'm going to be burying bodies by the end of the fucking day if she's walking around dressed like this.

Raking my eyes down her body, I audibly groan. She's wearing a pencil skirt, a black pencil skirt with white pinstripes; a slit runs all the way up her left thigh. I can see the top of her black thigh-high stockings, my cock instantly hardening as I picture those tanned, toned thighs wrapped around my head.

"Fuck, Ella! Did you leave half of your outfit at home? Because this cannot be all of it," I say, pointing up and down her body. I don't miss her nipples hardening, that poor excuse of a top doing nothing to hide them.

Ella notices where my gaze has stopped. She shivers. "Don't flatter yourself, Dean. I'm not a naive eighteen-year-old anymore. It's fucking cold in here."

I smirk at her; there is no way she's not turned on right now. I can see the rosy hue come to her cheeks, her pupils dilating. Tilting my head as I inspect her further, I watch her thighs tightening together. I smirk down at her. "Sure, babe, if that's what you need to tell yourself."

I shrug before leaning in and whispering in her ear, "But you and I both know, if I was to stick my hand in your panties right now, you'd be fucking drenched." I straighten.

Ella makes a point to look behind me; she smiles up at me as she says, "Well, I mean, he *is* really hot."

I'm going to kill him. I'm turning around to do just that as Zac shouts out, "What the fuck is going on in here?" My best mate has always had a knack for timing. I turn and smile at Ella. I'm not going to have to kill him now. Zac's here and I'm sure he'll have no issue breaking his whole *do things by the book* code. When it comes to his little sister, there is no fucking book.

"Either of you want to tell me why one of my employees is currently on the floor, whining like a little bitch?" Zac asks as he steps over Shawn without a second glance at him.

"Sure, mate. Shawn here, thought he could touch something that didn't belong to him." I nod my head in Ella's direction, so he knows that something is Ella.

I can see the moment it registers in his brain — his features harden. This is the look he gets right before a kill. Well, used to get; we haven't done things that way for years. I'd happily go back to killing, to burying bodies right now though.

"Don't be an ass, Dean. Zac, that's not what it was. We were just talking, when your goon over here came and knocked him to the ground." Ella pushes past me, walking up to her brother.

Zac's eyebrows go up to his hairline when he gets a full view of her. He looks over to me, catching me staring at her fucking delicious heart-shaped ass, her skirt wrapped around it like a glove. I don't apologise or back down from his stare.

Ella's a grown ass woman now, and she is fucking mine. Nobody will be keeping me from her. I'll always be loyal to Zac, but Ella comes first — she always fucking has — even if I did have to break her heart four years ago.

I did that shit for her, not me. She deserved to have the experiences of university, of being a new adult, without me dragging her down. Now though, I want nothing more than to drag her to my bed and tie her fucking ass to it.

After what feels like an eternity, Zac looks back to his sister. "Ella, where the fuck are the rest of your clothes?" He shakes out of his jacket and attempts to wrap it around her shoulders, which she dodges.

I watch as she straightens her spine, ready to go toe-to-toe with her brother. "Zac, I will walk out of this door and not look back if you think you're going to be treating me like a child. I'm here to work, not to be bossed around by the likes of you two," she asserts, pointing to us both.

I smile as I watch her stand up for herself. I've always admired her spark. Now though, I couldn't be prouder of her. I fucking love her determination, her strength.

"Oh, and Dean?" she smiles.

"Yeah, Princess?" The nickname I gave her — the name I've never actually said out loud in front of anyone other than her — slips freely from my mouth. It catches her off guard. Zac's gaze spears into me, questions and doubt in his eyes.

"Who I choose to let touch me has absolutely nothing to do with you. If I want to let your whole security team touch me, I will." Her voice is sweet as she gives me a glare, dropping the saccharine smile from earlier. "Oh, and drop the fucking 'Princess'. I'm not anyone's Princess, asshole," she says as she storms off.

"Hey, Ella!" Zac shouts.

She turns to look at him, waiting for him to continue. However, Zac doesn't continue his sentence. He walks across the room and over to the DJ equipment. Picking up a microphone and turning some switches on, he looks at her, smirks and then speaks into the microphone.

"Listen up, fuckers." He waits so that everyone in the room, which now includes the whole security team who have come out to be spectators of the show we've been giving, is listening.

"Any of you even think about touching my sister, you're fired. Anyone who lets another man touch her, without putting a stop to that shit, is fired." He points over to Ella. "That woman there is Ella, my little sister. Treat her as if she's your own sister and we won't have any problems. Understand?"

The fucker looks directly at me for that last part. I refuse to acknowledge the question. I won't lie to my best friend. I also won't deny that I plan to do very unsisterly things to Ella. I stand there and fold my arms over my chest, refusing to budge from his stare down.

Ella huffs as she walks out of the room. I'm thankful she's walking towards the lifts, and not the front door, like she threatened to do just minutes before. I want to chase after her and let her know just how wrong she is. She thinks I don't have a say over her body, over who touches her fucking body. It's laughable really. She's going to have to learn real quick that her body is mine. Her heart is mine; her fucking soul is MINE! That lesson is going to have to wait though. I have a mess to clean up here first.

It's been a long-ass fucking day. Ella has gone out of her way to avoid me as much as possible, mostly locking herself away in Zac's office. Zac has purposely had me doing shit on the floor. Every time I make it to his office, he's quick to get me out of there. It's only a matter of time before he confronts me about Ella.

I'm ready for it though. Maybe I should just come clean to him first, beat him to it. I'm currently sitting in his office, whisky in hand. Ella's been hiding out in the bathroom for the last twenty minutes. I'm not sure if she's listening or just waiting to hear me leave before she comes back out. I can hear the shower running, maybe she's just taking a shower.

I'm about to confess to Zac, to tell my best friend that I'm in love with his little sister. Tell him that I plan to keep her and there's not a damn fucking thing he can do about it. As I'm contemplating my words, Bray barges into the office, shocking both Zac and me. Bray hardly ever comes to the club anymore. He's been busy building his own empire these days — not to mention being a dad and husband.

"Good to see you haven't mastered the skill of knocking," I say to him. To which, he just flips me off as he walks to the bathroom door. He doesn't say a word to either Zac or me. Knocking on the door, he calls out, "Ella, it's me. Open the door."

The door opens slightly. Bray pushes himself inside before shutting the door, then I hear the sound of the lock clicking in place. Why the fuck is he locking himself in a bathroom with Ella?

"What the fuck is going on?" I ask Zac.

"No fucking clue," he says as he bangs on the door. "Bray, what the fuck's going on in there?" he yells.

Bray opens the door a crack, sticking his head out. He glares at me before telling Zac, "Ella's sick. She's not working tonight. I'm taking her home. I need you two fuckers to back up and give her some fucking space."

She's been fine all day. What the hell could she be sick with now? Bray's about to close the door when I stick my foot out, stopping it from closing.

"What's wrong with her? She's been fine all day," I ask.

"None of your fucking business. Stay the fuck

away from her!" he shouts in my face. Most men would walk away from a confrontation with Bray. I'm not most men though. I push the door open further and walk into the bathroom. What I see, though, has my blood running cold. What the fuck?

Chapter Three

Ella

I'VE SPENT the day following Zac around, being his shadow, and learning everything I can possibly learn about the club, while avoiding Dean as much as I possibly can. I couldn't get away from him quick enough this morning.

The fact that he was right, that I was so turned on just by being so close to him — having him whispering in my ear, his woodsy scent surrounding me, his touch sending jolts of lightning throughout my whole body — I felt like I was burning up from the inside. And he knew it. He knew the effect he had on me.

Then I remembered him walking out on me four years ago, leaving me broken and sobbing on my bed. I remembered the months I spent waiting for him to tell me he made a mistake, waiting for him to come back and claim me, to take me as his own.

That's when I found my inner rage. I let that shit boil to the surface and let him have it. I'm stubborn and there is no way I am going to come back and let him try to control my life, like he didn't leave me a mess of broken pieces.

He used to call me his Princess; now I'm just the broken Princess. Not his, not anyone's, just broken. And I don't know how to fix myself. I thought I had it under control. I thought I was finally beating it — this need to inflict pain on myself. The need to cut, I've fought it successfully for six months.

I'm itching in my own skin at the moment. I know I should tell Zac I need to leave. I should just go home or go to the gym, somewhere other than this place. I can't. I need to suck it up and get on with it. I'm here to do a job. I'm going to prove to Zac that I can handle this, that I can take over for him.

It's hard being back in this club, the place it all started. Images of the night I was attacked play in my head on repeat all day. I've avoided going up to the VIP floor. I know I'll have to face it eventually; there is no way I can avoid that floor forever. Just like I know I can't avoid *him* forever. Although I sure am going to try my best.

"Are you sure you're okay?" Zac questions me for the millionth time today. It's nine p.m. The club is just starting to get busy. I'm not on the floor. I'm just watching the camera feeds from the wall of screens in Zac's office.

"Yes, I'm fine, but if you don't stop asking me, I might not be," I grit out.

Truth is, I'm not okay… I'm far from okay. I'm not about to admit that to Zac, especially not on the first day of the new job. I'm going to suck it up, and get out of here as soon as I can. I plan on hitting the gym as soon as I get home.

Sitting on the couch, with my MacBook on my lap, I'm looking over the spreadsheets of last year's, which Zac sent me. Something is off with them, but he hasn't figured out where they're going wrong. Whatever is wrong with them, I'm making it my mission to figure it out, before Zac does.

I know I'm a little competitive. I also want to prove that I deserve this job. I may have gotten it because I'm family, but family or not, Zac would never keep someone on his payroll if they didn't deserve to be there.

Just as I'm getting comfortable, and sinking into the numbers, *he* walks in. Dean swaggers in like he owns the joint. He looks directly at me, his gaze intense, searing through me, and burning me up from the inside. I try my hardest not to squirm, not to fidget. *Do not let the lion know you're afraid.* That's what he looks like right now, a goddamn lion about to pounce on his prey. His prey being me!

Nope, not going to happen. I will not roll over and be his prey, be the thing he decided is good enough to play with now. Maybe it's all in my head again… I'm reading too much into his looks, into his words. I've probably conjured the whole thing up from my wanton imagination. I wasn't good enough four years ago, I'm certainly not good enough for him now.

I need to get out of here. Throwing my laptop on the couch, I head for the bathroom, locking the door behind me. It's so quiet in here. Too quiet. I pace up and down the small space for a few minutes before the quietness of the room starts to become too much, and the walls start to close in on me.

I turn on the shower, the white noise of the running water somewhat soothing. Also, if Zac hears the shower running, he won't wonder why I'm in here so long.

Sitting on the floor with my knees pulled up to my chest, I'm staring at the tiny razor I'm currently holding between my fingers. I can feel the pain already, just one little slice and I can escape these thoughts in my head. I want to do it so badly, my hands shake. Tears run freely down my face.

I can't take it. If I just do one little cut, that won't be so bad. I can just do a little bit and then everything will feel better. This is what I'm telling myself in my head. There's another voice though, a quieter one. This one is telling me no, don't do it. It's only my first day here. How do I expect to cope in this place if I'm curled up in a ball, and locked in the bathroom, on my first fucking day?

Through my foggy haze, I know what I need to

do. I need to call Bray. He will be able to help; he's always able to help me. Taking my phone out, I press the green button next to his name. He answers straight away, like he was waiting for my call.

"Ella, how's it being the big boss lady?" His voice is cheerful, but I can hear the undertone of worry there. It's always there, ever since he first caught me cutting a few years ago.

This time, that worry is warranted. I suck in a deep breath before whispering into the phone, "Bray, I… I need… I need help. I… I can't."

"Where are you? I'm coming now, Sweetheart. Where are you?" I hear the jostle of keys and the shuffling sounds of him moving around.

"I'm… I… in Zac's bathroom. Bray it's bad. I… I really want to right now." I try to explain to him how badly I want to cut right now. Maybe I should just do it. It would be easier to give in to the temptation.

"Ella, I know you want to. But you can do this. How long?" he asks, reminding me just how long it's been.

"Six months," I whisper.

"That's right. You are stronger than this, Sweetheart. I'm almost there. I'll be there in five minutes. Where the fuck is Zac?"

"Please, Bray, you can't tell him. Don't tell him." I'm crying into the phone, begging him to keep this secret.

Bray exhales loudly. I can hear the engine of his

car roaring. "Okay, I'm not going to tell. But, Ella, it might be time to talk to him about it soon."

"I know, just… not yet. I'm not ready."

"I'm pulling in now. I'm going to hang up. I'll be up there in a sec. Ella, wait for me in the bathroom. Do not move, okay, Sweetheart? I'm almost there."

"Okay," I agree, not sure where he thinks I'd go.

It feels like an eternity before I hear him knock on the door. Crawling over to the door, I flick the lock and open it slightly, letting him in. I crawl back to the corner I was in, curl my knees back up to my chest, and continue to stare at the damn razor in my hand.

Bray locks the door, squats down in front of me and plucks the razor out of my hand, putting it in his pocket. He tilts my chin up so I'm looking at him.

"You did it, Sweetheart. You fought it. You did it," he whispers as he pulls me into his arms, squeezing the life out of me. I always feel so safe here. My brothers have been my lifeline for as long as I can remember. But Bray, the last few years, he has been everything. Sometimes I worry that I'm taking too much. He has his own family. He should be at home right now with Reilly and the twins, not stuck in this bathroom dealing with my shit.

"I'm sorry." I cry into his chest.

It's not long before Zac is banging the door down. "Please don't tell him," I plead with Bray. Bray kisses my forehead. "I won't say anything. I promise." He stands and goes over to the door. I listen to the arguing between Bray, Zac and Dean. This is my fault; they wouldn't need to argue if it wasn't for me.

I'm still sitting on the floor, my legs still tucked up to my chest, and tears still running down my face. I hear a commotion and as I look up, I stare into a pair of blue eyes. The same blue eyes that haunt my dreams. The same blue eyes that sear deep into my soul.

Dean stops in his tracks. He stares down at me, his mouth open and shock evident on his face. He doesn't say anything. He doesn't need to. I know what he's seeing. He's seeing the broken mess that I am. I can't handle the look in his eyes—that look of pity. The questions running through his mind, I can see them all.

I look past him, somehow finding the strength I need to stand up. "Bray, can you take me home please?"

"What the fuck's going on? Ella, what happened?" Zac questions. I shake my head. I can't answer him.

Bray grabs my hand and pulls me past both Dean and Zac. "Come on, Sweetheart. I have a set of twins who are going to love seeing their favourite aunty when they wake in the morning."

"Bray, I swear to God, you'd better start talking. What. The. Fuck. Is. Wrong?" Zac demands.

"Chat later, Bro. Things to do, people to see, you know how it is." He looks at Zac, like he's communicating messages with his eyes. Zac looks at me, worry all over his face. He gives the slightest nod. I make the mistake of looking behind him at Dean. He hasn't said a word, nothing. He's still just staring at me like he can't figure out what he's seeing.

I wake up to shouting. Zac and Bray are downstairs shouting at each other. "Argh." I pull a pillow over my head. "Make them stop." Nobody is here to hear my protests. What the hell are they arguing about now? As the sleep fog slowly clears from my head, memories of last night hit me all at once. Fuck, they're arguing over me. I should get up and go fix the mess I've created. I probably should have stayed in Melbourne. Maybe it's not too late to go back.

I throw the pillow off my head. I'm going to have to face the music. I might as well get up and get it over with. Sitting up, I slowly open my eyes. I wipe the blur away, a little gasp escaping my mouth, as my eyes focus on the figure sitting on the end of the bed.

A very large figure, with familiar blue eyes staring into my bloody soul. Anger rises up to the surface.

What gives him the right to be sitting in here, watching me fucking sleep, like a creeper?

"What the hell, Dean? What the fuck are you doing in here?" I whisper harshly at him, while pulling the blanket up to my chin.

His eyes follow the blanket as I yank it up, a smirk pulling at his lips. That fucking smirk never fails to make me wet. Damn it. Where the hell did my anger go? I have to dig down deep to pull it back to the surface. It doesn't take long, considering he still hasn't answered my damn question.

"What are you doing here, Dean?"

"What happened last night?" he questions me back.

"No," I say, shaking my head.

Dean's eyebrows scrunch. "No, what do you mean no?"

"I mean no. No, you don't get to come in here asking questions. No, you don't need to know what happened last night because it's none of your fucking business, Dean!" Well, that anger sure is back tenfold now. I'm ready to wrap my hands around his throat and choke the life out of him. How dare he come in here thinking he can demand answers.

He smiles at me; the bastard looks like he is holding in a laugh. "That's quite the potty mouth you've got on you there, Princess," he says, smiling like a fool.

"First, not your Princess. Second, what the fuck

are you smiling about?" I ask, my hands itching to slap the smile from his face.

"You're really fucking cute when you're mad, Princess. Keep swearing at me all you want. Your filthy mouth only turns me on. I'm currently thinking of the ways I'm going to fill it, before washing it out with my seed and cleansing the filthy with filthy." He shrugs.

My mouth hangs open. Did he really just say that to me? He just said he's going to shove his cock in my mouth. Why the hell is that image in my head turning me on so much? Damn him. Before I can even get my bearings, he starts talking again.

"Oh, and Princess," he says moving forward, grabbing my chin in his hand, and forcing my eyes to meet his. "Whatever concerns you is very much my business. You are my business. Don't think for a second I won't throw you over my shoulder, carry you out of this house, take you home and tie you to my bed until I get the answers I want."

"Mmm." My hands fly up to cover my mouth. Shit! I can't believe I just let that moan escape. So much for my *you don't affect me* attitude. But, boy does the idea of being tied to his bed sound good. No, it's not going to happen. I need to think with my head, not with my heart or that traitorous bitch of a vagina I have. She wants nothing more than for me to spread my legs wide open and offer a warm, wet place for his cock to live.

"Argh!" No, I can't do this. I need to get away

from him. Pushing the blanket off, I stand up. I am just about at the door when a big beefy arm wraps around my waist, picking my feet up off the floor. The next thing I know, I'm flying through the air and landing back on the bed that I just climbed out of.

Chapter Four

Dean

I LOOK DOWN at her spread out on the bed, her dark brown hair above her. She's a fucking goddess, her tiny shorts and tank top doing little to cover her golden skin. My mouth waters at the sight of her nipples pebbled under her tank, her mouth open in an O shape from the shock of being thrown down on the bed.

This is a look I could get used to seeing. I wonder if her mouth makes that same shape when she's out of her mind with pleasure — pleasure I plan on giving her daily.

Jumping up on the bed before she recovers from her shock, I straddle her hips, then reach up, grab her wrists and pin them above her head.

"There is no way in hell you're walking out of this

room dressed like this, Princess. You might as well be walking around naked."

I nuzzle my face into the side of her neck. She struggles underneath me, trying to free herself from my hold. She's not getting free. I won't be letting her go anytime soon.

"There's no one here other than my brothers, idiot. Pretty sure they're not going to be staring at my ass," she hisses. "Let me go, before you fucking hurt yourself, old man."

I laugh, which only pisses her off more. "I let you go once, Princess. It was the hardest thing I've ever had to do. I won't be doing it again."

The struggle leaves her. Her body goes limp under me as she stares up, her eyes shiny with unshed tears. It fucking breaks my heart, the lost look that glazes over her eyes.

Shaking her head, she whispers, "You didn't let me go. You left me. To let someone go, they have to want to be freed. I did not. No, you left me, broke me, and now, I'm nothing but a broken piece of who I used to be."

I swipe the stray tear that falls down her cheek with my thumb, my other hand grasping both of her wrists together. "There is nothing broken or imperfect about you, Princess. I did the right thing. I did what was right for you. I chose you over myself. You think it didn't fucking shatter me to walk away from you, to give you the freedom to live a little without being tied down to someone like me?" I ask.

Trailing my lips up the side of her neck, I whisper promises into her ear — promises I should have fucking told her four years ago. "I wish I could take it back. I wish I had kept you. But I've got you now, Princess. You are mine, and I'm not letting you go, no matter how much you fight me."

My fingers trail up and down her wrists. My body freezes when I feel them. I look up and see the countless little scars that decorate both sides of her wrists. She tries to pull her hands away, tries to cover up. That's not going to fucking happen.

It all happens so fast; her breathing increases. I can feel the erratic beat of her heart; her body becomes covered in sweat. She's shaking her head no. "I… I can't breathe. Dean, I… I can't."

She's having a fucking panic attack. I sit up, bringing her with me, and cradle her in my arms. "It's okay. You're okay, Ella. Just breathe, in and out." She follows my direction as she breathes in and out, burying her head into my chest. I don't move. I just continue to whisper in her ear, to rub my hand up and down her back. I feel fucking helpless right now. And like an ass, for making her have a fucking panic attack.

Once I feel her body relax, I ask, "You good now?"

She nods her head as she moves off my lap. The only reason I let her go is because I don't want to cause her to panic anymore. I watch her every move, ready to catch her if she falls again.

Ella crawls up to the head of the bed, sitting with her legs drawn up to her chest. This is how she was last night in the bathroom. I should have picked her up and walked out with her then. Seeing her like this shocked me stupid. I don't know what to do. I don't know what is wrong with her. Is this my fault? I can't help but think I actually did fucking break her… *Fuck.*

I sit next to her, grab hold of her hand and intertwine our fingers together. Then I wait. As much as I want fucking answers, I know I can't push her, can't add anymore extra pressure or stress to her already heightened levels.

After ten minutes, yes, ten minutes — I've been watching the fucking minutes on the clock, tick minute by minute — I have to know. "It's my fault, isn't it?"

Ella looks at me, sadness in her eyes. "It's not your fault, Dean. I have panic attacks, that's all. It's nobody's fault. That's what was wrong with me last night. That's why Bray came to get me."

Panic attacks do not explain the scars on her arms. As much as I want to know about them, I can tell she's not ready to answer those questions. "How long have you been having panic attacks, Ella?" I ask, fearing I already know the answer.

"Since the night you left me," she answers honestly. "But they're not that bad anymore. I don't have them as often anymore. It was just being back in the club. I guess I thought I would handle it better."

"I'm so sorry I did this to you. I'm never going to

fucking forgive myself." What the fuck have I done? I thought I was doing the right thing by leaving her. She's needed me all this time and has not once reached out.

"Why didn't you call? You know I would have come. I'd do anything for you, Ella. All you have to do is ask."

"I asked you not to leave me, and you did." She tries to pull her hand free of mine. I grip tighter.

"I didn't leave you. I gave you time. I thought I was doing the right thing."

Ella shrugs. "Well, you weren't. And you can't just come in here and think everything is hunky-dory. It's not okay. I'm not okay. Now you know I'm broken."

"I don't think that we're going to pick up where we left off. We have shit to work out, like dealing with your fucking brothers. But you are mine, and I'm not about to let anyone get in the way of us again."

Leaning in, I do what I've wanted to do for four years. I claim her mouth. I lick the seam of her lips and push my way inside, invading her mouth with my tongue. She doesn't return the kiss for a few seconds; then, out of nowhere, her tongue duels with mine. Before I know it, she's climbing on top of me, strad-dling me.

My hands go straight to her ass. God, I've wanted to get my hands on this ass for so fucking long. I let her take control, let her think she's in control for a little while. She grinds her pussy down on my cock. *Fuck*. "Argh," I groan as I break away from the kiss.

"Fuck, Princess, as much as it pains me to say this right now, we need..."

My words are cut off when she slams her mouth back onto mine, aggressively. She's taking what she wants, and I'm prepared to give it all to her. Just not right now, with her fucking brothers still arguing downstairs. I pull back again; she grunts in disapproval.

"Princess, I want to do this. I really fucking do, just not with your brothers right downstairs." I kiss her forehead. I can't read the look that crosses her face. She tries to move off me. Wrapping my arms around her waist, I pull her body tighter against mine. I lift my hips so my rock-hard fucking cock grinds into her clit.

Ella's gasps are music to my ears. Her little moans, like a fucking symphony. "Feel that?" I grit out through clenched teeth. She nods her head.

"That's all for you, because of you. My cock is fucking hard and I'm in danger of coming in my pants right now, because of how much he wants to be buried inside of your cunt. This is happening, Ella. *It will happen*. Just not right now."

I kiss her gently, hoping she gets the message. Just because I'm not an asshole and taking her for the first time in her brother's house, does not fucking mean she is any less mine.

"Okay," she says shyly. "I should probably go downstairs and sort them out anyway." I let her climb off me.

"Do me a favour, Princess. Put some fucking clothes on before you walk out that door." Standing, I make no attempt to hide the fact that I'm adjusting my cock in my pants. Her eyes dart down, the slightest blush creeping up her tanned cheeks.

"Just so you know, I was already planning on having a shower and getting dressed. I'm not changing because you told me to." Stomping her way into the bathroom, she slams the door behind her. God, I've always loved her spark. Now to go deal with the shitstorm that's about to go down when I tell them that Ella is mine.

I make my way downstairs; I don't try to hide the fact that I snuck up there in the first place. Both Zac and Bray are going at it in the living room. "You realise both of you fuckers woke her up with all your fucking yelling, right?" I have to yell to be heard over the top of both of them.

Ever had two grizzly bears turn on you at once? Yeah, me neither, but I imagine this is what it fucking feels like. Both Williamson brothers spin and aim their deathly glares straight at me.

Bray looks up at the staircase, where I just came from, then back to me. Without a word, he walks up and throws a fist right to my jaw. Fuck, he's got a good right hook. As much as it fucking hurt, I'm not about to start throwing down with him. Well, not here anyway. In a gym, far away from Ella, sure. I know he didn't put his all into that punch; he held back. When I look up at him, he smirks at me, before yelling out a bunch of random curse words that would make a sailor blush. This is exactly where Ella gets her filthy mouth from.

He finally stops cursing, then says, "Good to see you finally found your balls, asshole. Is she okay?" He nods his head in the direction of the stairs. I give a slight nod. This fucker knows whatever the fuck Ella is going through and he hasn't said anything. I squint my eyes at him. I'm about to ask him how long he's known for, and what exactly it is that he knows… Does he know she's been self-harming? Because that's the only thing I can think of that would explain all those tiny, thin scars up and down her wrists.

But I'm interrupted by the barrel of a Glock being pointed at my head. I'm not scared. He won't shoot me. At least, I'm pretty sure he won't. I know him as well as I know myself, so I'm ninety percent sure the fucker won't shoot.

"Why the fuck are you still carrying around a Glock?" I ask. Bray goes to stand in front of me.

"Bro, put that thing away," Bray says to Zac as I shove him out of the way.

"Get your ass out of the way. We are not watching you sleep for another two months when you get yourself shot again." I have to put more effort into moving his huge ass.

"Give me one good reason why I shouldn't shoot you right now?" Zac growls at me.

Chapter Five

Ella

I MAKE quick work of showering and dressing. I do take my time applying makeup to my wrist, ensuring it's blended well. I still can't believe Dean saw them. I don't let anyone see them, ever. I'm usually so careful with covering these scars up. I held my breath waiting for Dean to ask about them.

He never asked though. He didn't question me about my panic attack. He simply sat with me, held my hand and waited. Dean's always had a way of comforting me and making me feel safe. I wasn't sure I'd ever feel that way again, until he held me in his arms, whispering promises of a future in my ear.

I want to believe him. I want to give in and take that chance. But he broke me once. I will not survive that again. I'm still not recovered from four years ago. I don't think I ever will be. How does someone move on from having their heart ripped from their chest?

I want to let him claim me and see where it goes. I want him just as much as I did four years ago, maybe even more. I've been in love with him since I was fifteen. I tried everything to get him to notice me, to get him to want me. Then I was attacked, and he was my saviour.

He spent the next two months sneaking into my bedroom every night. He held me as I cried myself to sleep on his chest. I know he was feeling something for me, something more than just the platonic feelings. He was seeing me as more than just his best friend's little sister. The asshole just wouldn't act on it. He chose his friendship with Zac over me, at least that's what it felt like at the time.

Now, he's here, claiming that I'm his — whatever that even means? Do I want to be his? Fuck yes, I do. I want it more than anything. I want him more than anything I've ever wanted, especially after that kiss. I felt like I couldn't get enough of him. I literally wanted to crawl into his skin, to invade his nervous system like he was invading mine.

I almost came apart when I felt his hardness underneath me. I know I'm inexperienced at this, at sex. I've been kissed before, back in high school, but I've never let another man touch me. I tried to date a few times at uni, but I just couldn't do it. They weren't *him*. Will he still want me when he finds out just how inexperienced I am? What about when he really discovers how broken I am? He saw a mild panic attack. How's he going to respond when he knows what I do to myself?

Why can't anything in my life ever be easy? I'm torn from my inner torment by the yelling downstairs. I'm going to have to go and face the music eventually. I might as well get it over with. When I say music, I mean Zac. I know I have to face him. I know how he's going to react too. That's exactly why I made Bray promise not to tell him.

I stomp down the stairs, my stomach dropping when I see what all the commotion is about. Zac is currently pointing a gun at Dean. Images of seeing Bray in that hospital bed after being shot run through my mind. No, this is not happening again.

"Give me one good reason why I shouldn't shoot you right now?" Zac directs, unflinching, with his features hard as stone. He looks like he would actually shoot him, without a care in the world. I've never been afraid of my brothers, but right now, Zac is scaring the ever-loving crap out of me.

"Because I fucking love her, man. You can shoot me. It won't change anything though. She will always be mine, no matter what the fuck you fuckers do."

My steps freeze. He loves me. Well, it would have been fucking nice for him to tell me that before he told my brothers. Men are such idiots, clueless fucking idiots.

"How long have you been fucking my sister

behind my back? I fucking trusted you, asshole!" Zac yells.

Stomping forward, I go to walk past Dean and Bray. I plan on walking up to Zac and slapping the fuck out of him. How dare he speak about me like that. How dare he point a gun at Dean. Dean's strong arms wrap around my waist, stopping my movements, and attempt to pull me back behind him. I smile.

Bray laughs. "Well, *this*, I can't wait to see." He rubs his hands together. Dean doesn't know that I'm not the helpless little girl I used to be. When he had me pinned to the bed earlier, I pretended to fight. I didn't actually want to get out from under him. I let him think I was weak. I should feel bad for what I'm about to do. I don't though.

Bringing my left foot down, I stomp as hard as I can. I should feel bad, that I'm about to hurt him, but once again I don't. No amount of physical pain will equate to the emotional turmoil I've been suffering from for the last four years. Also, I've spent many hours watching Dean and Bray train together. I know he can handle anything I dish out.

Bending at the waist, I pull down on his arm. Taking him down with me, I have the power of surprise right now, so I use that to my advantage. He's not expecting this. I use his own weight against him as I flip him over. He lands harshly on his back.

I look down with a smile on my face; his shocked expression brings me way more joy than it should. I don't waste time. I know he will recover and jump back up. Jumping over his body, I go up to Zac and pull the Glock out of his hands. He is in just as much shock as Dean. Meanwhile, Bray is laughing his ass off.

Removing the magazine, I use my thumb to pop out fourteen rounds, each one landing on the floor at Zac's feet. Once the magazine's empty, I cock the slide and eject the round from the chamber. Then I hand both the gun and the magazine back to Zac with a smile on my face.

"Don't ever pull a gun on a family member again, asshole." Turning to face Bray and Dean, who is now on his feet with a huge ass grin on his face, I ask, "So which one of you wants to take me out for breakfast? Because I'm starving."

"Sorry, Sis, no can do. I need to go meet Reilly at the gym. The girls are running wild on her."

Dean screws his face up at Bray and shakes his head. "As if I was going to let you be the one to take her anyway. Princess, let's go." He holds his hand out for me to take. I look from his face to his hand as he waits for my decision.

After a minute, I take his outstretched hand. His fingers entwine with mine. It feels right. It feels natural, like we've been holding hands forever. There's a growl from behind me, then the unmistakable cursing of Zac. "Deal with that, can you, please?" I say to Bray as I walk past. I don't look back as I walk towards the door, hand in hand with Dean.

"Ella. Wait," Bray calls out.

Turning, I look at him and wait. I know what he's going to say.

"How long?"

"Six months." I smile and walk out the door.

THE CAR RIDE to the café was silent. Dean held my hand the whole way, his thumb rubbing small circles around my wrist. I tried to pull my hand away. I knew he would be able to feel the scars I work so hard to hide. He just gripped my hand tighter, refusing to let go.

Now, sitting here in the café and overlooking the Sydney Harbour, we are in a comfortable silence as we both look over the menu. The sun is shining down on the water. Large white yachts fill the harbour; they have a peaceful look to them. To be out on the water, sailing off into the sunset, seems like a pretty good way to spend the day.

"What are you in the mood to eat?" I ask him. I can't decide. Maybe he will have a good idea.

Dean chuckles. "Princess, what I want to eat is not on the menu."

Okay, so I'm not the quickest today; it took me a good minute to realise what he was referring to. When I do, my eyes widen and my cheeks get hot. Thank god that my olive skin hides the redness that would otherwise be very prominent right now.

"Ah, well. Um…" Shit, I have nothing. I don't know how to reply to that. *At all.* "Have you ever thought about buying a yacht?" I blurt out randomly.

Dean's eyes light up as he laughs. "A yacht? I already have one," he says so casually, like it's not a big fucking deal to have a yacht.

"When did you get a yacht? And are we talking a pimping kind of yacht, or a little rowboat you call a yacht?" I ask curiously.

"It's not a rowboat. I inherited it from my dad. I'll take you out on it one day."

"Okay, so I'm thinking pancakes," I announce, folding the menu back up and placing it on the table.

The waitress comes up to the table, briefly looking at me, before giving Dean bloody goo-goo eyes. *Um, hello, Malibu Barbie. I'm right here.* I don't like the jealous, possessive feelings I have running through me right now. It's irrational. I pick up my butter knife, gripping it tightly. I'm running through all the ways I can possibly use this knife right now without anyone noticing.

I'm about to slide the knife under the table… I just need to feel a scratch. I need to escape these feelings. I can do a little scratch on my thigh; no one will notice. At least, usually no one would notice. Dean reaches over the table, grabbing hold of the hand that is currently gripping the knife like my life depends on it.

"What was it you said you wanted, babe?" he asks, not breaking eye contact with me.

I loosen the grip I have on the knife, slightly; my eyes water as I stare into his. How does he read me so well? How did he know what I was going to do?

"Uh, pancakes, with cream and strawberries," I whisper. Dean smiles at me.

"Two servings of pancakes with cream and berries. One Mocha and one strong black. Thank you." Dean dismisses the waitress. I wait for the questions to start coming as soon as the waitress walks away. I don't know how to answer them, but I can see the questions in his eyes.

Chapter Six

Dean

I WATCH as Ella wraps her hand around the knife, grasping it tightly, her knuckles turning white with the force. Her eyes glaze over, like she's zoned out. I'm not sure what has caused her mood to change so drastically. I'm also not one hundred percent sure if she's planning on using that knife to gut the waitress she's staring daggers at, or on herself.

I have a hunch, a really fucking good hunch, how she came to get all those scars on her arms, and I'm sure if I inspect her body more thoroughly, I will see a lot more. As she slowly begins to drag the knife towards her, it's clear she's attempting to get it off the table without drawing attention to it. *Not gutting the waitress then.*

Fuck, I reach out and grab hold of her hand. Squeezing tight, I stop her from removing the knife from the table. No fucking way will I sit here and let her hurt herself. I need to draw her out of her own mind. I rub circles around her hand with my thumb, in an attempt to soothe her.

"What was it you said you wanted, babe?" I prompt, my eyes never leaving hers. I try to convey that I know, that I want to help her. She just has to want me to help. She whispers that she wants pancakes.

I tell the waitress what we want, without breaking eye contact with Ella. Once the girl walks away, I feel Ella's hand loosen its grip on the knife. Her whole body relaxes slightly. She's still staring at me with a look of uncertainty, waiting for whatever I'm about to say.

The conversation we need to have is not one that needs to happen at a fucking café. I need to put her more at ease, to change the tone back to the fun first date this should be.

"Tell me about university?" I ask.

Ella looks back in shock, over the fact that that's the question I asked. "What do you want to know?"

"Everything. I never got to go, so I want to know everything. Who were your friends? What did you do for fun? What subjects did you like the most? What did you hate the most? Like I said, everything."

"Everything?" she repeats. "You want me to tell you about the last four years of my life over pancakes?"

"Well, mostly everything. Feel free to leave out any

and all information pertaining to boyfriends. I do not want to fucking know that." My jaw tenses as I grit out the words. Thinking about Ella with other men makes me want to punch myself. Because that would be all my own doing. I was the fucking idiot who pushed her away.

"Well, that's easy, because there haven't been any." She shrugs her shoulders. She's unable to make eye contact. I can't help the fucking huge-ass smile that greets my lips. I'm about to tell her how happy that fucking makes me when the waitress comes back, plops the two coffee orders on the table and walks away in a huff.

"Princess, look at me." I wait until her eyes meet mine. There's really no point beating around the bush. I need to know. I blurt out the question that's burning the tip of my tongue. "Are you a virgin?"

The question takes her by surprise; her mouth opens and closes. I hold my breath waiting for her answer. She looks around the café before looking back at me.

"Dean, you cannot ask me that in a fucking café!" she hisses.

"Why the fuck not? Answer the question, Princess, or I'll ask it again. Only louder." I raise the volume of my voice slightly. I don't give a fuck who hears me.

"Okay, shut up. Yes, I am. Are you happy now? Are there any other invasive questions you feel the need to ask over fucking breakfast?" She crosses her arms over her chest, my eyes following her movements as her breasts push up. Fuck. She's fucking gorgeous when she's mad.

"Yes, I'm fucking ecstatic actually. To know I'm going to be the first and only man to enter your pussy. That makes me a very happy fucking man." To know that she's untouched, that she hasn't been with anyone… I can't describe the feeling, only one word comes to mind. Mine.

"You're pretty sure of yourself. What makes you think I'm going to let you into my panties? Four years ago, I would have jumped at the chance. But I'm not a little kid anymore. I grew up, and trust me when I say this. I have no plans of letting you fuck me anytime soon."

Fucking hell. I have to adjust my cock in my jeans. Hearing those words from her mouth… *fuck me*. Those fucking words made my cock instantly hard.

"Besides, how do you know I don't have my sights set on someone else. This is Sydney. There are a lot of fine fish in this sea." She waves her arms around.

There goes my boner. "Princess, if you let any fucker touch you, you might as well be signing their death certificates. Because I will fucking kill them. I will tear them limb from fucking limb. I'll gut them like a fish, reach into their chest and rip their fucking heart out with my bare hands."

Ella screws her face up at me. I'm surprised that she's not disgusted with my promises of violence. "Well, that's… graphic and slightly disturbing. You can't actually be serious."

The waitress again interrupts our conversation, when she comes over and places two plates of pancake stacks on the table. I wait for her to disappear before I speak again.

"Are you prepared to test the theory? Because I can assure you, Princess, I am deadly serious."

"Uh, okay." She tilts her head as she thinks. "Does Zac know you have these psychotic thoughts, by any chance?"

"Why?" I am not going to be the one to tell her that her big brother, who she fucking idolises, is crazier than Bray and me put together. That's saying something, because Bray's a fucking crazy bastard with no fear. Even after being shot and left in a coma for two months, the fucker has no fear.Except for his ridiculous fucking fear of flying. Get him on a plane and you'd think the world was fucking ending.

Ella picks up her fork and reaches out on the other side of her plate for her knife. She lifts the plate looking underneath it, as if somehow the knife would be under there.

"Huh, where'd my knife go?" she asks, as she bends down and looks under the table.

"You mean this one?" I hold up her knife, which I swiftly swiped without her noticing.

"Did you…? How? Why? How'd you take that without me even seeing? And why would you take it?"

"I have skills. You'd be surprised what I can do with these fingers." Holding up my hands, I wriggle said fingers in her face.

"Okay. Well, eat up before they get cold." Using her fork, she points to the pancakes. We both eat in silence for the remainder of breakfast. I finish mine long before she does hers. It's fucking torture sitting here watching her eat, listening to her little fucking moans as she chews the syrupy goodness. I wonder if that's what she'll sound like when I drink her syrupy goodness straight from her pussy.

As she licks her fingers clean, she smirks at me, sucking each finger into her mouth one by one. I want to reach over the table, grab those fingers and suck the syrup off myself. I also want those delicious fucking lips of hers sucking on something much bigger and wider than her fingers.

"Just curious, if I do decide I'm going to let you hang around me, how much backlash will Zac dish out? Obviously he knows you better than anyone, so if he knows you're fucking bonkers, there is no way in hell he's letting you near me. He already pulled a gun on you today. How long do you think until he pulls the trigger?"

"You're wrong, you know."

"About what?"

"Zac's not the one who truly knows me. You are."

Ella shakes her head no. "I've hardly seen you in the last four years. I feel like I barely know you anymore." The lie slips off her tongue with ease. The way she diverts her eyes, the little tick in her jaw... That's her tell. That's how I know she's full of fucking shit.

Standing up, I drop some cash down on the table and reach my hand out to Ella. She doesn't hesitate to take it. I love the warm feel of her hand in mine, the sparks that run up my arm as my fingers entwine with hers. It's like no high I've ever felt. She can try to deny it, but I know she feels it too.

Shutting the passenger door, I walk around the front of the car. After I pull out of the carpark, I take Ella's hand in mine and place it on my lap. I'm turning into a fucking girl, but I like holding her fucking hand.

"Where are we going?" Ella asks as she looks around my car. "And why the hell does everyone have a nicer car than me?"

I laugh. She has a one-hundred-and-eighty-thou-sand-dollar car. I know how much it was because I was there when Zac bought it for her. "Ella, your car is plenty fucking nice, but if you want a new one, I'll buy you one."

"I have a trust fund, you know, and a job now. I'm

more than capable of buying my own car."

"Just because you *can*, doesn't mean I *can't* buy one for you."

"Okay, don't take this the wrong way. I'm totally aware that what I'm about to ask is rude and crosses every social rule. But I'm curious. Where do you get your money from? I know this particular car is around three-hundred-and-fifty-thousand dollars. You work in security. It does not add up."

"First, there is no question you can't ask me. Those social rules do not apply to us. Second, I don't take a fucking cent from your brother for the job I do. I do that job because you Williamsons are the family I choose. I'd do anything for any one of you."

"You know that we love you too, right? There is no way Zac would have pulled that trigger," she says with shiny tears.

"You love me, huh?"

"Shut up, idiot. You know I fucking do. I have since I was fifteen."

My face hurts from how hard I'm fucking smiling right now.

"You can wipe the smile off your face. Just because I love you, does not mean I'm letting you into my panties."

"Well, just in case you weren't sure, I fucking love the shit out of you. I know I stuffed up. I know we have work to do to build us up. But there is no other option, Princess. You are mine. We both know it."

"So, where does a volunteer security worker get

enough cash to buy a car like this?"

"You really don't know? Zac never mentioned it?" I ask. How have I known this girl since she was eleven, and she does not know who my family is?

"Know what? Wait, are you secretly a mob boss? Are you taking me back to your compound now, to lock me up and never let me out?" she asks, almost as if she wants that to be the truth. I almost wish that it was the truth.

"You read way too many books. But thanks for the idea; it's oddly appealing. No, I'm not a mob boss. I'm a McKinley. I get my money from old family money."

Ella's mouth drops open. I knew as soon as I dropped my last name, she would connect the dots. I fucking hate being a McKinley. I'm definitely the black sheep of the family, my mother's greatest disappointment.

"Holy shit, Dean! How the hell have I never known your last name? How the hell did I not know you're a fucking McKinley? Wait, we are talking about *the* McKinleys, right? As in the ones who own all the shit around Sydney and have all those racehorses and crap?"

I grit my teeth. Don't get me wrong, I love my mother. *In small doses*. She is my mother after all. She's also a fucking stuck-up bitch with a pole up her ass.

"Yep, those McKinleys. Well, there aren't too many of us. My father passed away a few years back. Now it's just my brother, me and my mum."

"I'm sorry about your dad. Why haven't I ever

heard you talk about your family?"

"Don't be sorry. I'm not. He was not a good man. And, because when I was young, the moment people found out who I was, they expected shit. The only exception was Zac. When he found out who my family was, he shook his head and said *you poor bastard.* That was that; we were best mates ever since."

"Okay. Well, you know I don't want anything from you, right? I don't even know if I want *you* yet."

"I know." I squeeze her hand. "Also, Princess, stop fucking lying. You're no good at it."

"Where are we going anyway? You never answered me."

I smile. "Home. I'm taking you home."

"Uh, my apartment is in the other direction. This is not the way home, Dean."

"We're not going to the apartment. We're going home, as in my home, which is now going to be your home."

"Ah, I don't even know what to say to that. Did you forget to take your crazy pills this morning? Because I'm pretty sure you just asked — no, not asked — you just declared that I was moving in with you. That's not how this works. You can't just make a decision and decide for both of us."

"Babe, relax. You are my home. Wherever you are is where I am. And wherever you are is my home. Whatever building that may be, I don't fucking care. But there will not be a night, from now on, where you are not in my fucking bed."

Chapter Seven

Ella

"HOLY FUCKING SHIT, DEAN!" I yell as I crane my head out the window. What the fuck is this? He has to be kidding, right? He does not live here. Why would he not invite us over for a dinner party or some shit. Well, I mean, it's Dean, of course he's not hosting dinner parties.

"Is it a hotel? Wait, you don't secretly have a harem of women in there waiting for you, do you? Because you can't possibly live here alone." I'm rambling, I know. But damn. This fucking house.

It's three stories high. There's a large wrap-around veranda on the bottom floor, and balconies on the other two floors.

A row of white pillar columns line the front of the house. Dean pulls the car around at the front house, jumps out and opens my door. I know I can open it myself, but I grew up with Zac and Bray always getting cross at me whenever I did. So, now it's easier to wait.

"Thank you," I say, taking Dean's outstretched hand. No sooner than he shuts my door, a man appears, like poof, out of thin air. Where the hell did he come from?

"Good morning, Sir," he directs at Dean with a, "Ma'am," to me. Do I look old enough to be a ma'am? As I'm debating this, Dean introduces me.

"Geoffrey, this is Ella. Ella, Geoffrey. Ella's going to be around a lot; whatever she wants see to it that she gets it," Dean says as he pulls me towards the house.

"Ah, no, Geoffrey you do not need to do that. I won't be around that much anyway."

Geoffrey laughs before coughing into his hand. "Of course, Sir, whatever she wants," he affirms before getting into the car. I don't see where he goes in it. The wind gets knocked out of me as Dean bends then throws me over his shoulder.

"What the hell are you doing?" I yell. "Put me down."

"I'm carrying you across the threshold. That's what you're meant to fucking do. Be quiet."

"That's when you get married, idiot. We are not married. Put me down."

"Yet, we are not married yet. But we will be. How's next Tuesday work for you?"

I laugh, because he made a joke. Except, he's not

laughing. I can't actually ever remember a time when Dean made a joke. "I'm busy." I finally get out.

"Doing what?" he asks as he opens the front door.

"Washing my fucking hair." A loud smack rings out through the room. Then I feel it, the sting radiating from my ass. The delicious burn, the slight twinge of pain. A small moan escapes my mouth before I can stop it. It's a nice kind of pain. I feel tingly sensations running through me.

As I'm trying to process how I'm feeling about this slight pain, I realise I don't have the brain fog, the haze I usually get when I cut. It's different. Why is it different? Don't get me wrong, I'm loving this feeling, the freeness. I can't describe it. When I feel pain, my brain quiets down, my body tingles in pleasure. But this… although I'm tingling, my mind is clearly not quiet. I don't understand it, and that scares the shit out of me.

I land on my feet, my heels clanking on the floor. Dean holds onto my arms, steadying me. Once I'm satisfied that I'm not about to fall on my ass, I pull myself out of his grasp. Spinning around in a circle, I look up.

My mind is going a million miles per hour, trying to process the pain sensations, as well as what my eyes are seeing right now.

We are standing in what looks like the setting of a Hollywood movie. I'm in the middle of the entryway. To my left, there is a staircase with black metal balustrades, to my right, the exact same thing. He has two staircases. Grand does not even come close to describing this entryway. From above, a large chandelier hangs right down the centre.

Taking a step forward, my heels clank on the floor. Looking down at the white marble flooring, there is a huge fucking family emblem in the centre of the entryway, all fancy in black and standing out against the white.

I come from a wealthy family. Before my parents died, we certainly were not poor by any means. When Zac took custody of me, he had doubled my trust by the time I received it at twenty-one. But this, Dean and his family, this is another level of money. This isn't just money; this is the goddamn bank.

I'm about to walk ahead, to go explore, when Dean pulls on my arm, dragging me behind him and up the stairs. "I'll give you the tour later. Right now, we've got shit to discuss."

"Ah, okay." My voice comes out a little uncertain. What the fuck does he want to discuss? I'm praying it's not my scars, which I know he saw. I also know he feels them as he rubs his thumb up and down my wrist. No matter how much I try to pull away from his touch, his grip just gets firmer.

Dean drags me into a bedroom. He shuts the door behind him as I look around. Clearly, this is more than just a bedroom. This is like an apartment all of its own. It's also got Dean written all over it. I take a few steps further into the room.

There's a huge sitting area with four single sofas

facing each other. Why would anyone need four sofas in their bedroom? It's all dark and gloomy in here. Maybe he should try going for some lighter colours. The sofas are black, with dark navy cushions. A glass coffee table sits in the middle of them.

The bed? It's huge. I bet you could easily fit five adults on it and still have room. Dark navy, fluffy-looking bedding covers the bed. The room is meticulously clean. I honestly didn't peg Dean as a neat freak.

Walking past the sofas and bed, I head to the far corner. There's a bar there. Now, that does seem very Dean-like. Walking behind the bar, I pop open a bottle of Jack and pour myself a glass. Some liquid courage could be a good thing right now. Dean stands at the door, just watching me. It's unnerving. He's also blocking the only exit from the room, which has my skin crawling and not in a good way.

I pour another glass and as I bring it to my mouth, it's ripped out of my hands. Dean downs it, before slamming the glass back down on the bar.

"Let's play a game," Dean says as he picks up the bottle, grabs another glass and pours two drinks.

"Okay, what game?"

"Twenty Questions. I'll go first." He hands me the drink. He waits for me to bring the glass to my lips and take a sip, before he asks his question. "When did you start harming yourself?"

I choke on my drink. That was not what I was expecting his first question to be. I don't even know how to respond to that. How do I tell him that I started before I left for university?

"I, um… a few years." There's no point denying it. He should know the level of instability and broken that I am.

"Why do you do it?" He asks his second question.

"Uh, no, it's my turn. Why didn't you ever have us over here for a dinner party?" Jeez, that's what I ask? Out of all the things I could have asked…

Dean laughs. "I don't do dinner parties. That's more my mother's scene. And trust me when I say, you're not missing out by not going to them."

"Well, I just don't get it. You live in this big house, by yourself. You do live here by yourself, right? Of course you do. Why didn't you ever invite me over?"

"Zac and Bray have both been here. You were barely eighteen when you went to uni. If I had brought you here, did what I wanted to do to you back then, your brothers most certainly would have killed me."

"What did you want to do to me?" I ask.

"Nope, it's my turn. Why do you need to inflict pain on yourself?"

"I'm going to need another drink. Okay. This is not something I've talked about to anyone other than Bray and my therapist."

"Babe, there is nothing you can say that will change this. This, us, it's fate. You can't break fate." I want to believe him, but I don't know if there is such a thing as fate.

"I'm really messed up, Dean. I'm broken. I cut myself to escape the thoughts in my own head. When the noise gets so loud, I can't cope. The memories so vivid… The only way I was able to quiet them was to cut. I don't know why. It was an accident the first time it happened. But when I do, I feel more at ease. I feel more peace than any other time. Almost any other time."

I can feel the tears running down my face. "I understand if you want me to leave. I can call Bray; he'll come get me." I'm giving him an out.

"You're not fucking leaving, Ella. We are going to talk about this. I don't care how broken you think you are. I happen to think your kind of broken is my kind of perfection."

"You don't know how broken I am yet, Dean."

"And you don't understand the extent I'm willing to go for you."

Chapter Eight

Dean

ELLA TIPS HER HEAD SIDEWAYS, those deep brown eyes of hers searching for truth behind my words. She can search all she fucking wants. She won't find anything but the truth.

"Why now? Why do you all of a sudden want me now? When four years ago you left me. You fucking left me, asshole! You walked out without even a second glance." Her voice raising, she throws her glass across the room. It shatters as it hits a wall, broken shards falling to the ground.

I don't move. I don't flinch. If she needs a fucking punching bag, I'm more than happy to be it. Besides, I deserve her anger. I deserve her distrust.

I watch her movements as she starts pacing the room, ready to catch her if she attempts to walk out that door. She can be angry; she can curse me out all she wants. What she can't do, what I won't allow her to do, is fucking leave.

"You ripped out my fucking heart and stomped all over it!" she yells as she starts throwing the books from the coffee table at me. She misses every time. One thing Ella has never been any good at is ball sports. She can't aim for shit, never has been able to.

I stay quiet, watching. She's like a caged animal, all of her rage towards me coming to the surface. After years of being stamped down, she can finally let it out. Then hopefully let it the fuck go.

"I would have done anything to be with you back then. Why? Why the fuck did you walk away from me?" She flips the glass coffee table over, letting out a frustrated scream when it doesn't break.

Turning around, she looks at me — stares me straight in the eye — as she whispers, "I fucking needed you. I needed you and you left me." Her words destroy whatever was left of my soul. What the fuck did I do to the one woman I've always loved?

She falls to the ground sobbing. Seeing her like this, seeing what I fucking did to her, it's wrecking me. I walk over to her, bend down and pick her up. Settling her in my lap, I cradle her head to my chest and let her cry.

I don't know how long we sit like this for. My legs are numb, but there is no way I'm moving, no fucking way I am letting go of her. I don't even notice that I, too, am crying until she looks up at me with red-rimmed eyes. She reaches her thumb up to my cheek and wipes away my tears.

This beautiful fucking creature in my arms, crying her heart out because of what I did to her, still wants to comfort me.

"I will never be able to tell you how fucking sorry I am. I promise to do everything in my power, every day, for the rest of our fucking lives to make it up to you. To show you just how much I fucking love you. I love every little thing about you, Ella. Always have. Always will."

Turning her around so she's straddling me, I grab her face and slam my lips down on hers. Her soft, plump lips are even softer from her tears, a salty taste lingering on her lips. Plunging my tongue inside of her mouth, I groan, as our tongues entwine together. I can't seem to get close enough. I need more. I need it all. I try to convey in this kiss just how much I fucking love her, try to show her with my touch how fucking special she is to me.

Standing up, I carry her into the bathroom. I don't stop kissing up and down her face, her neck, anywhere my lips can reach. Reaching into the shower, I turn it on; water falls from the ceiling. I don't wait for the water to warm.

Stepping in, I slam her against the wall of the shower. The water cascades down us both, cleansing us, washing away the past and baptising us with a fresh future.

With her legs wrapped around my waist, and her

hands running through my hair, my cock strains in my now soaking-wet jeans, aching to be released. To find its home. Grinding into her pussy, I savour how she moans in my mouth, the cotton of her dress sticking to her skin and showcasing all of her soft curves. I need to get rid of these fucking clothes.

Walking to the seat at the other end of the shower, I sit her down. Squatting down in front of her, I slowly lift her dress. Our eyes connect. Our souls connect, the way they always have been. She doesn't stop me as I lift the dress. As the wet fabric slides up to her chest, her arms lift. I rip the dress over her head and throw it behind me.

Falling to my knees, I'm speechless as I stare at the fucking goddess in front of me. Beautiful, golden skin. Curves in all the right fucking places. She's wearing black lace, and she wears it so fucking well. Her chest heaves up and down with her breathing, her breasts popping out. I can see her nipples through the lace of her bra. They're calling to me, begging me to give them the attention they deserve.

"You are so fucking gorgeous, Princess. Your body is an untouched canvas I want to paint with my goddamn tongue. You are nothing but perfection." I'm so mesmerised in all that she is. I could sit here and stare at this beauty all fucking day. My tongue waters as my gaze travels down, her pussy on full display through the thin black lace of her panties.

She starts to close her legs. *That's not fucking happening.* That little bit of black lace is doing nothing to cover her pussy. I can't wait to get a taste of that. I want to fucking devour her. I move closer, placing my body between her thighs, preventing them from closing. I'm on my knees in front of my queen, exactly how it should be.

My hands travel up the smooth skin of her legs, up her sides, and around her back. Using one hand, I unclasp her bra and watch as the straps fall down her shoulders. Ella takes a big breath in as she pulls the straps all the way down her arms — her breast free with her hard nipples right in front of my fucking mouth.

I don't waste any time. Moving in, I wrap my mouth around her right breast. My tongue swirls around her nipple, and her body arches, pushing her breast even further into my face. Her hands tentatively go to the back of my head, her fingers twirling in my hair.

I grasp her other breast in my hand, tweaking the hard bud before pulling and twisting slightly. Her moans fill the room, echoing off the walls. It's the best fucking sound ever. My mouth moves, switching between breasts and showing each one just enough attention to get her worked up. I wonder if I can make her come from just nipple play. By the way her body is arching, her legs tensing and trying to close, and her pussy rubbing against my stomach, I don't doubt she would come apart like this.

That's not how I want to give her, her first orgasm. No, I want that to be on my tongue. I want to lick every drop of her juice. Her hands grasp the hem of my shirt, bringing it up. Pulling away from her breast, I tug the shirt over the back of my head. Her hands travel up and down my chest, and around my back tentatively, her fingers so soft.

Shivers wave through my body at her touch, my skin alight. If she keeps this up, I'm going to embarrass myself and come in my fucking pants, like a thirteen-year-old.

With a slight growl, I rip her panties, pushing them aside. I bend my head down, holding each of her thighs in my hands. I don't give her time to think or to protest what I'm about to do. I just dive in. Dive in and fucking drown.

My tongue swipes from the bottom to the top. Her body arches off the seat. My grip on her thighs tightens, keeping her right where I fucking want her. I swirl my tongue around her clit; she screams out in pleasure.

I pump my tongue in her entrance, fucking her with my mouth. Her hands grip my hair, pulling my head away, and then pushing me closer. Moving back to her clit, I suck it into my mouth and nibble with my teeth. She's so fucking close.

I insert two fingers inside her wet pussy. I know, I'm an asshole. I should use only one. She's untouched, but I can't help it. She's so fucking tight, wet and warm on my fingers. Two pumps of my fingers and she's coming undone. Her body tenses, and her head falls back, hitting the wall.

Her legs quiver as she rides out the high of her orgasm. I lick every last drop of her release. She's the best fucking meal I've ever eaten. I plan on making this a daily requirement. Fuck, I could eat her for breakfast, lunch and dinner and still not get enough.

Once I feel her body relax, I remove my fingers. Bringing them to my mouth, I moan around the taste left on them. She smiles down at me shyly, innocently. Ella Williamson will be my undoing. In fact, I think she already is. Always has been. Always will be.

Chapter Nine

Ella

HOLY FUCKING SHIT! What the hell just happened? What was that? Okay, clearly, I know what it was. It was the best fucking orgasm I've ever had. Considering up until this very moment, every other orgasm I've had has been from my battery-operated friend that lives in my bedside drawer, it's probably not a lot of competition. But Fuck.

My body feels like I'm floating. Opening my eyes, I look down at Dean, who is staring at me with an odd expression. I smile, albeit awkwardly. What does one say after being given the orgasm of all orgasms? It dawns on me that I am completely naked.

Naked! In front of Dean. My brother's best friend. The same guy I've been in love with since forever. How many times have I had this dream? Countless. I pinch myself on the arm. Ouch, yep, I felt that. Dean's eyes follow my movements.

"I'm not dreaming, am I?" I ask.

He laughs, a full-belly kind of laugh. It's the contagious kind of laugh. "No, Princess, you're not dreaming. You are a fucking dream! My Dream."

"Oh, okay. Well, uh… Thank you?" My gratitude comes out as more of a question than a statement.

"Thank you? What the fuck are you thanking me for?" Dean asks, his eyebrows drawn in confusion.

"For… you know. That thing you just did," I say quietly. I can feel my face heating up. Why do I have to pick now to lose my cool?

"No thanks required, babe. That was my pleasure, a fucking privilege. One I'm going to be taking advantage of as often as possible."

He stands up, the outline of his hard-on evident through his wet jeans. My lips suddenly dry, I swipe my tongue along my bottom lip. Dean growls then lifts me up from under my arms.

"No, do not fucking look at me like that, Ella. I'm holding on by a thread here," he grits out between clenched teeth.

"Like what?"

"Like you want me to shove my cock down your throat. Thrust in and out of your pretty little mouth until you're swallowing my seed."

I don't even know what to say to that except, "Well, it's not an unappealing picture you just painted."

Dean lets out a string of curses, before he steps out of his shoes and pulls his wet socks off his feet. Damn it, why do his feet even have to be attractive? My eyes travel up his body unashamedly. I watch as his hands unbutton his jeans and he pulls them down, stepping out while leaving himself in a pair of black briefs.

My hands itch to pull them down, to free his hard-on, which I can very clearly see. At the same time, it scares the shit out of me. That thing does not look little. As I'm contemplating this, Dean pulls me under the water, running his hands through my hair.

He then places me just out of the water's reach. Picking up a bottle from the shelf, he squirts liquid into his hands. I watch as he brings his hands to my head. He starts massaging the liquid, which I now assume is shampoo, into my hair. I close my eyes, inhaling the scent. He's washing my hair with his shampoo. It's been a long time since anyone, other than a hairdresser, has washed my hair for me. The last person to wash my hair with this much tenderness was my mum. She had her own salon chair set up in our house; she would take me in there and wash my hair as she sang along, albeit badly, to Cher songs.

She used to tell me she loved my hair so much. She always wished she had hair as thick and beautiful. She'd tell me that, one day, I would have a daughter of my own, with dark hair and dark eyes. I got my eyes from my dad, whereas my brothers got their green eyes from our mum, who had lighter features.

A tear slips from my eyes before I can stop it. Dean's quick to notice; he bends and kisses the tear away. Then he moves me back under the water and washes the soap out of my hair.

Dean takes his time as he washes my body with a loofah. It's clearly a richy-rich loofah because I've never felt anything like this. No loofah I've ever had has been this soft. By the time he's finished, my body is alive with electricity. My core is pulsing, seeking... something.

I take the loofah out of his hands. This, I'm going to enjoy. I smile up at him.

"Lose the briefs." My voice leaves no room for argument. It's time to even the playing field.

Dean smirks before pulling his briefs down his legs and kicking them to the side. I can't help my mouth dropping open when I finally see what's been straining to get free. His cock — long and hard — stands, touching his belly button. The head of his cock leaking pre-cum, all I can think — is how badly I want to lick it off.

"Does that hurt?" I'm genuinely curious; his face is scrunched up like he's in pain.

"Like you wouldn't fucking believe. I want nothing more than to bend you over and slam my cock into your pussy. Filling you up, entwining our bodies until we are one." He shakes his head.

"But that's not happening right now. The first time I make love to you is not going to be a quickie in the fucking shower."

"Okay." Squirting soap on the loofah, I start to wash over his shoulders, then his arms. I work my way down his rock-hard abs. He really is moulded out of stone. My free hand follows the path of the loofah. The feel of his skin under my fingertips sends sparks flying up my arms. My stomach fills with butterflies.

I can't believe I finally have Dean in front of me. *Naked*. Mine for the taking. And I don't have the faintest fucking clue what to do with him. How do I pleasure him like he did me? I feel way out of my depth. His chest rises, his breathing getting heavier. His eyes droop as he watches the trail of my hands. He doesn't say anything. He stays perfectly still as my hands explore what they have been itching to touch for years.

I make my way down to his cock. He hisses as I rub the loofah over the top. Gripping him with my free hand, I gently rub up his length. He wraps one of his hands around mine, squeezing tight and stopping my movements.

"You don't have to do that, Ella," he whispers. I can see how turned on he is right now. I want to do this. I want to be able to please him, to pleasure him.

"I know I don't have to. I want to. Do you not want me to touch you?" I ask, looking down at where our hands are joined over his cock, unsure I can handle it if he says no.

He lifts my chin until my eyes meet his. "Of course I want you to touch me. I just want you to know that you don't have to. I don't want you to do anything you think I want. I want you to be comfortable. Shit, I don't know. I don't want to screw this up again, Ella. I want to take this at your pace."

"Well, I want to do this. So, show me how. Show me how to pleasure you, Dean."

"Fuck," he grunts. "Okay, squeeze tighter, like this. Move your hand up and down."

Dean's hand stays over the top of mine, guiding me on the amount of pressure and speed. His head leans back, his eyes closed. "Fuck, Ella, just like that. Keep doing that," he says as he removes his own hand.

His hands start roaming over my body. I continue to explore, gripping firmly and swirling my thumb around the head of his cock, as I pump him up and down. It doesn't take long before he lets out a string of curses. He wraps a hand over mine and points his cock in my direction.

Next thing I know, he's coming all over my stomach, spraying his seed over me. *Marking me*. When he's done, he claims my mouth. His tongue pushes its way into mine. I smile, happy that I could actually make him come apart like that. Seeing him lose himself in pleasure, yeah, I need to see that again. Soon. I wrap my arms around his neck and pull his head closer to mine. I can't seem to get close enough. Jumping up, I wrap my legs around his waist. He catches me, his hands digging into my ass.

I'm pretty sure I'm going to be left with fingerprint bruises from how hard his fingers dig in. I moan into his mouth, pressing my core into his cock. Sparks fly. I continue to rub my clit over his length, which is still rock hard.

I'm chasing that high again; it's so fucking close. Dean pushes me against the wall, my back hitting the cold tile as he grinds into me. One of his hands comes up and pinches my nipple. At the same time, he bites down on my shoulder.

The pain from the bite sets me off. I don't just fly over the edge, I fucking soar. I scream out his name as I come. Once the fog leaves, I realise what just happened. The pain, mixed with pleasure, that just took me to a higher level of any high I've ever felt from cutting. It scares the shit out of me, because I think I may have just found a new addiction.

I look into his eyes. Does he know what just happened? Can he tell how screwed up I am? Is he going to want to throw my ass out the door now? There are so many questions running through my mind.

"I fucking love you, Ella Williamson. Always have. Always will," he finally says, his voice hoarse. He leans in and kisses me so softly on the lips.

"I fucking love you, Dean McKinley. Always have. Always will," I repeat back.

Dean washes me off again. He then wraps me in what has to be the world's softest towel, before carrying me to the bed. We lie together in the middle of his huge-ass fucking bed, a sheet covering our naked bodies.

A girl could definitely get used to these kinds of sheets. They're probably something ridiculous like a million-thread count. Lying here with my head on Dean's chest, my leg draped over his body, this is bliss. The silence surrounding us is comfortable. His fingers run up and down my back. His heartbeat is steady under my ear.

"Do you have cameras in this room?" I ask.

"Uh, no, why?" He's cautious with his answer. I wonder if that means there are cameras in other rooms. There would have to be.

"No reason." I shrug. Looking up at him, I add, "But if these sheets happen to go missing, it wasn't me."

Dean laughs, his body shaking mine. He probably

thinks I'm joking. I'm not. I will find a way to steal these sheets.

"What time is it?" I ask. I have no idea how long we were in that shower for. Or how long we have been lying here like this.

Dean reaches over to his phone, cursing when he swipes the screen on. "It's two o'clock. Shit, Princess, we have to leave the bubble."

I give him my best pout. "But I like the bubble."

Dean leans down and kisses me gently before he rolls me off him. He lands on top of me. Mmm, this is a much better position.

"I love this bubble. But we both have to get to the club. You're going to be late. You know how much your brother loves it when people are late."

At the mention of the club, I jump. Or, at least, I try to jump. It's not an easy task when you have a six-foot something beast of a man on top of you. When I shove at his chest, he gives in and lets me up.

"Fuck, Dean, I have no fucking clothes. My dress is wet." Picking up the towel, I wrap it around my body.

"As much as I love this towel, which also, if it goes missing, it wasn't me, this isn't going to go over too well if this is what I have to wear to the club." I wave one hand over my body.

"It's fucking funny that you think I would let you walk out that door in that towel, Princess. You really should consider becoming a stand-up comedian," Dean deadpans.

"Yeah? It's funny you think you would have a say in what I wear," I challenge back.

Dean just smirks at me, grabs my hand and pulls me towards a door. When he opens it, he lets me go in first. "I'm sure you'll be able to find something in here."

"What the fuck!" I am standing in a walk-in wardrobe. Although it could very well be another bedroom, it's that fucking huge. But it's what's in the wardrobe that has my blood boiling. It's full of clothes. *Women's clothing.* There's one wall that's full of shoes. Heels in every colour, it's like a rainbow wall of fucking shoes. Rows of handbags line the shelves.

"What the fuck is this, Dean? Why the hell do you have a wardrobe full of women's clothes? Oh fuck, you're not fucking married, are you?" Just my luck, to fall for the guy who's married and cheating on his wife. *With me!*

"What the hell are you talking about? You know damn well I'm not fucking married. This is yours. It's all brand new. I had it purchased for you. As soon as I knew you were coming home." He almost looks uncertain — it's a look that flashes by quickly — before the confident smirk reappears.

"You bought all of this for me?" I ask. "Why?"

"I wanted you to have stuff here. For times like this. You need clothes, Ella. You're not fucking walking out in a goddamn towel. Besides, I had help. So, I'm sure you will find something in here you like."

"You had help? From who?" I cross my arms over

my chest. Why does the thought of someone else helping him make me so mad with jealousy?

"Reilly. Who else is going to volunteer to willingly do all this shopping? And she assured me you'd like it."

Reilly. I smile. I know Reilly's taste exactly. And it's good. She has great taste, and it's usually always very revealing. "Okay, I'll get dressed. Go. You need clothes too." I push him out the door, shutting it behind him.

"Why do I feel like you gave in way too fucking easily then, Princess?"

"Because I did. Don't get used to it. It won't happen often."

I run my hands along the racks of dresses. My eyes land on a silver sequined dress. It's shiny, and form fitting. I open drawers until I find what I need, the drawer full of lingerie. Picking out a pair of white lace panties, I'm quick to get dressed.

The dress fits like a glove, leaving absolutely nothing to the imagination. I love it. I send a little thank you to Reilly as I hunt for a light jacket to throw on top. I do not want Dean to see this until we're already in the club. By then, it'll be too late. He can't object. And he might think twice about letting Reilly loose with his credit card again.

I find a beige cotton coat that falls to my knees, I pick up a pair of black Louboutins and slip my feet in. At the end of this ridiculous wardrobe is a vanity table with all sorts of cosmetics laid out.

Rummaging through the various bottles of lotions and potions, I find some leave-in conditioner. I lather it in my hair. I don't have time to do anything else to it. It's unruly and wavy, like I just got out of bed, which is fitting. I did just get out of bed after all.

Settling for some red lipstick and mascara, I take one last look in the mirror at my reflection. I know it's not work attire, but I work in a nightclub, and this is most certainly nightclub attire.

"Okay, I'm ready," I call out as I walk out. My eyes roam up and down Dean's body. He's wearing navy blue dress pants with a white business shirt. He's folded the sleeves of the shirt up to his elbows, showcasing those delicious forearms.

"Are you sure you want to wear that?" I ask. Don't get me wrong, he looks hot as hell. That's the issue. Every girl who enters that club will be eyeing him.

"Why, what's wrong with it?" he asks, looking down at his clothing.

"Nothing! That's the point." I throw my hands up. "Let's just go get this over with."

I don't even make it to the door before Dean grabs my hand. "Whatever your brothers have to say, I will not let you go, Ella. You. Are. Mine."

"Okay. Don't worry, if Zac decides to pull a gun on you, I'll save you. *Again*." I laugh.

"Don't think I've forgotten about that little stunt you pulled. You caught me off guard once. There won't be a second time."

I laugh and follow him out to the car, each step

increasing my nerves over having to face Zac. Bray, I'm not so worried about. He already knows how I feel about Dean. He was worried that I would come back and fall apart at seeing Dean, fall back head over heels and not be able to be with him. He doesn't know I never fell out of love with him. In the back of my mind, I was always hoping, always waiting, for our time. This, now, it's our time.

Sitting in the car, holding Dean's hand, I whisper, "Always have. Always will." I didn't mean for him to hear it. But when he repeats the phrase, before kissing my hand, I know that he did.

Chapter Ten

Dean

I CAN FEEL Ella's nerves radiating off her. I can see her fidgeting with the belt on her coat. I'm not sure why she's wearing a coat in fucking October. Surely she's not cold, unless she's getting sick.

"Are you sick?" I blurt out.

"Uh, no." Shaking her head, she looks at me, confused.

"Just checking," I say, shrugging like it wasn't an odd question to ask right now.

I know that Zac will see us the moment we walk into the club. There's no point in trying to avoid the situation. I might as well get it over with. I lead Ella to the back lifts, my hand firmly on her lower back. As much as I want to push her against the wall in the lift and smudge that red lipstick off her lips, I know at least one of her brothers is watching right now.

I don't need them engraving my name on the bullet. *If they haven't already.* It's got to be the slowest fucking trip up the lift.

"Are you nervous?" Ella asks.

"Not at all. Why would I be?" It's not like I have seen Zac kill men for much less crimes than dating his baby sister. Is that what this is? Dating? I feel like it's so much more than that.

"We should get married." There goes my mouth, blurting out every fucking thought around this girl. Any cool I had, flew out the fucking window a long time ago when it came to Ella.

"Ah, sure. When were you thinking? I think I have an opening on Tuesday at noon. Does that work for you?"

I honestly can't tell if she's joking or not. I was not. "It sure does, Princess. I'll book the courthouse." I make a mental note to do just that: book the courthouse for every Tuesday at noon for the next few months. I'm pretty sure she won't cave by this coming Tuesday. But one of them, she will.

Walking down the hallway, I lean down and whisper in her ear, "I can't fucking wait for you to be Mrs. McKinley."

She doesn't have time to reply before I shove open Zac's office door, only to be greeted by the squeals of women and kids.

Reilly and Lyssa run up to Ella, engulfing her in hugs while pulling her away from me. I scowl at them both. They don't notice.

"Aunty El! Aunty El!" Ash screams as he climbs down off his dad's desk and runs full speed to Ella. She bends down, catching him in her arms, as she picks him up and spins him around.

I'm so mesmerised by her, I don't notice the little red-headed bundle pulling on my leg. I pick her up and look at Reilly. "Is this twin one or twin two?" I ask. I can never tell them apart. I don't know how anybody does; they look exactly the same. It's either Lily or Hope.

"One," Reilly says, before turning back to Ella.

"Well, at least with this baby in my arms, I know Bray's sure as shit not throwing punches." I smirk down at the little drooling redhead, then walk towards the back of the office. I need to face these bastards.

"Sunshine, take Ash and the twins down to the bar. Get them some ice cream from the kitchen for a bit," Zac demands.

Lyssa laughs. She's probably the only one in the world who can get away with laughing at one of Zac's demands. Well, she, Ella and Reilly. He and Reilly developed some weird fucking relationship when Bray was in a coma. They went from hating each other to practically braiding each other's hair.

"Not a chance, babe. You are not running poor Dean over the coals because he finally grew a pair and admitted he was in love with Ella."

"What the fuck, you knew too? Am I the only fucking idiot that didn't know this was going on?" Zac asks, pointing between Ella and me.

"Uh, first of all. Hang on. Ash, can you build Aunty El a castle?" Ella places Ash on the floor and runs to the corner, where there is a big basket of Legos.

"Okay, first of all. This." Ella points between herself and me. "Was not going on until today." She then starts to undo the belt on her coat. She continues talking to Zac as she shakes out of the coat.

"Second, language! There are young children here," she scolds.

Once she has that coat off, she throws it on the couch.

"What the fuck are you wearing?" I growl at the same time Zac and Bray do.

Ella looks towards me, which makes every other pair of eyes look towards me as well. "Don't you like it? I thought you wanted me to wear something out of that ridiculous closet you had put in your house for me?" She even goes as far as flashing those damn eyelashes at me.

"You are never getting near my credit cards again, Reilly. Take it back. Take it all fucking back. Fuck, donate it to charity. I don't give a shit. This is not a fucking dress, Reilly. It's a — I don't know what the fuck it is." I can't take my eyes off Ella; she's fucking stunning.

Standing there in a shiny silver dress, her hair a mess of waves down her shoulders with bright red kissable lips painted on her face, she's a fucking dream.

"You had a fucking closet put in your house for her. What the fuck, Dean? How long have you been planning this little charade of yours?" Zac yells.

Hope starts crying in Bray's arms. Bray glares at Zac.

"Don't worry, Hope, Uncle Zac is just a cranky old man. Don't listen to him," Bray coos as he bounces Hope up and down in his arms.

Zac walks over and plucks her from him. "Sorry, baby girl, but Uncle Dean has some kind of death wish," he says in a singsong voice, while rubbing circles on her tiny back.

Hope giggles; she has no idea what Zac's saying.

"Truthfully? You really want to know how long I've been in love with your sister?" I ask. The whole room goes quiet. All except Ella.

"Uh, Dean, he really doesn't need to know all the details. Some things are better left between us, you know." She's obviously worried and wary of Zac's reaction.

"Sure, might as well tell me how long my best fucking mate has been stabbing me in the back."

"Okay, stop your fucking sulking, Zac. He has not been stabbing you in the back. He wouldn't even touch me. I practically threw myself at him when I was eighteen and he walked away. So, no! He has been nothing but the most fucking loyal friend to you. Stupid, but loyal. You don't get to sit here and rip him apart." Ella is furious as she points her finger at Zac.

Bray walks over and takes Hope back. "I think I'll

take this one back. Have at it, Sis. He's all yours." He walks out of the way with a laugh.

"What do you mean you fucking threw yourself at him when you were eighteen? And why the fuck would you turn down my sister? Is she not good enough for your snooty ass? Not fucking well-bred enough for mummy?"

Okay, this fucker is losing his damn mind. First, he doesn't want me to touch his sister. Now, he's questioning why I didn't.

"She was fucking eighteen, Zac. Of course I wouldn't touch her. She had a great future ahead of her. Had university to go to. She needed to live. So, no, I didn't follow my fucking heart all those years ago. I thought I was doing the right thing by everyone. *Everyone*, but my fucking self. If I had known, I would have gone to Melbourne and dragged her ass back here years ago."

Ella gasps and shakes her head, tears forming in her eyes. "What's wrong?" I ask, reaching for her.

"They don't know. Please don't do this now," she whispers, begging. Looking around the room, I see it's already too late. No one in this room is going to let go what I just said.

"Fuck!" Bray dumps Hope in the stroller. He looks over his shoulder. "Babe, take the girls downstairs for ice cream." He pauses before he adds, "Please."

Reilly looks around the room before agreeing. "Sure, come on, Lyssa. I think Ash needs to teach his cousins how to eat ice cream without making a mess."

"Okay," Alyssa agrees. She engulfs Ella in a hug and whispers something in her ear.

As she's walking out the door, she stops, turns around and says to Zac, "Hunny, I am really attached to Dean. Try not to kill him." She blows him a kiss before walking out the door with Reilly and the kids.

"Fucking hell, now I can't just slit your damn throat like I was planning to." He smirks at me.

The fucker probably *was* planning to, probably had the knife picked out already.

"Uh, I think I'll just go with the girls." Ella tries to leave. Bray steps in her way.

"Not so fast, El."

"Brayden, if you do not move, I will give you a twin to the shiner you got there." She points to the slightly black and blue eye Bray has.

"You got lucky. This conversation is long overdue, El." He pulls her over to the lounge and sits down with her, still holding her hand.

I want to go and rip her away. I want to be the one holding her hand. I should have been the one holding her hand all these fucking years. But it was Bray she relied on... it was Bray she leaned on. I settle for sitting next to her.

I cup her chin and turn her face so she's looking at me. "Princess, Zac should have known about this a long time ago. This is not the sort of shit you keep from your family." I glare in Bray's direction. I'm fucking pissed he knew and didn't say anything.

"Zac, get the whisky and sit your fucking ass

down." I know him, which means I also know he is going to blame himself for what Ella has gone through. And he's going to want to fix it for her. She is like a daughter to him. He's raised her from the time she was thirteen.

"Someone better start fucking talking. What's going on?" he growls as he plops down on the couch opposite to where we are seated.

"I—I can't. Bray?" Ella looks pleadingly at Bray.

"Ella, sweetheart. Whatever it is, you can tell me. You know you can tell me anything. I can't help you if you don't tell me." Zac sits forward, his forearms resting on his legs.

Ella shakes her head no. "You can't help me, Zac. No one can."

"Fuck that. Princess, we are going to help you. We will get through this," I assert, my voice raising. I feel fucking helpless right now.

"Ella. Oh fuck. Are you pregnant?" Zac looks like he's ready to jump across the table and wring my neck.

"What? No. I'm not fucking pregnant, Zac. I'm still a goddamn virgin. Because I've been waiting four fucking years for Dean to wake up to himself!" she yells.

I can't help but smile at the fact she's untouched. I know I'm an asshole. I just don't care.

"Wipe that fucking smile off your face, asshole. That's still my sister." Zac points at me, then Ella. "Okay, not pregnant. Good. So, what is it? Are you in trouble? Do you need money? I've got plenty stashed away. How much do you need?"

"She doesn't need your money. She's not going to want money for the rest of her life. She's going to be a fucking McKinley," I growl. As much as I hate dropping my family name, and rarely fucking do, on this occasion, I'm more than happy to remind the asshole of who I am. Of what I have.

Bray spits out his drink. Zac squints his eyes at me. "You're serious about this, aren't you?"

"Deadly."

"Okay. Just how exactly do you plan on making her a McKinley without mummy interfering and vetoing this relationship? Because, let's face it, you and I both know she will."

He's probably right. My mother is going to have a coronary when she finds out I plan on marrying Ella, without a fucking prenup, mind you.

"Easy. We're getting married on a Tuesday at noon. At the courthouse." I smile.

Zac shakes his head. But I see the fucker trying to hide a smile. Maybe I will leave this room with my life intact?

"*She* happens to be right here. *She* is also not getting married anytime soon. So don't go getting any crazy ideas. Any of you," Ella says, pointing her finger at each of us individually.

"Okay, so what is it that these two buffoons seem to know that I don't?" Zac's impatience over not having the information is clear in the way his leg bounces up and down. It's the one and only tell of his frustration. Looking at his face, you'd think he was as cool as a cucumber.

"I… um… well, I have some things I've been working through over the past few years. But I'm better. I'm getting better. I promise. I am getting better, right, Bray?" Ella is so uncertain of herself. I want to pick her up and shield her from the fucking world.

"Yes, you are. How long?" Bray asks.

Ella smiles and says, "Six months."

"Six months since what?" Zac asks.

"Since I last cut myself… on purpose," Ella whispers, rubbing at her wrists. I grab hold of her hand, stopping her movements. She is not alone anymore. She needs to know that I am here, no matter what.

After sitting on that couch for an hour, listening to Ella retell her story to Zac (a lot of it, I was hearing for the first time), I want to fucking slit my own mother fucking throat. She should never have had to feel that alone. I should have been there, helping her.

Bray just took her downstairs to find the kids before they had to go home for the night. As soon as the door closed behind them, I rushed into the bathroom before emptying the contents of my stomach in the porcelain bowl.

Once I'm satisfied nothing else is coming up, I flush the toilet and sit back, leaning against the cabinet. Zac stands in the doorway. He throws a bottle of water at me.

"You good?" he asks.

"Not really," I answer honestly. He comes and sits down on the bathroom floor next to me.

"How could I not know? How did I not see that she was having trouble?" he asks.

"She didn't want you to see."

"I should have been able to tell. Fuck, she's been in Melbourne for four fucking years by herself. I'm meant to look after her, Dean. It's my job to fucking look after her." His head rests on his knees. I knew he wouldn't take this well. Fuck, I'm not fucking taking it well.

"I shouldn't have walked away from her. If I had stayed with her… If I had admitted to her back then how I felt, she wouldn't have even gone to fucking Melbourne."

"Maybe not, but four years ago, I would have fucking killed you for touching her."

"So, what I'm hearing is: *Dean, I'm not going to kill you for claiming my little sister.*" I smile at him.

"Fuck off. I'm still contemplating it. I just have to work out what accident you're going to have. Because if Alyssa or Ella find out I knocked you off, I'd be meeting you in Hell the next day." He laughs.

"Are we going to get through this?" I ask. "Because I love you, man. You're my best friend. But if you make me choose, I will choose her."

"We're family. Family works through their shit, without killing each other. *Usually*," he says. And that's good enough for me. "So, can I be there when you take her home to your other family. Because, that, I gotta see." He laughs.

"You know I won't let them anywhere near her, right? Besides, Mum has been strangely different since the old man carked it." I shrug.

"How so?"

"I don't know. It's hard to explain. But way less judgy and all up in my business. My mum almost sounds happy and sober, the few times I've spoken to her."

My mother would be what you'd call a functioning alcoholic. Anyone can function though, when you've got McKinley wealth behind you.

"That's good?" Zac questions.

"Yeah, it is."

"Okay, I gotta ask."

"What?"

"Are your intentions with my little sister pure? Are

you certain she's the one? The forever one. Because if you break her heart again, I will not think twice before ripping yours out and dishing it up to her on a plate."

"She is my always. I was serious about marrying her, you know. I asked her in the lift on the way up here. She thought I was joking."

"Okay, Romeo. So, let's figure out how to get her to marry your sorry ass. Because, as much as it pains me to say this, you are a good guy, Dean. I know you'll do right by her."

"That hurt, huh?" I laugh as I roll some of the tension out of my shoulders. I really need to get up off this fucking floor.

"You have no fucking idea how much," Zac grunts out.

Chapter Eleven

Ella

IT'S BEEN two weeks since I came home. Two weeks, since Dean and I have been able to be us. It's fucking bliss. That is, when Zac isn't hovering over me and treating me like a fragile piece of glass.

I've been putting up with it. Because he needs it. He needs to feel like he's helping me. I appreciate how much I am loved by him and Bray. A girl really could not ask for two better brothers.

It's the end of October. Tomorrow is my birthday. Usually, my brothers make a huge deal out of my birthday. They try to make up for our parents not being there for all my milestone birthdays. But this year, it's dead silent. Nothing. They haven't even mentioned it.

It's possible they've forgotten. They do both have children of their own, wives and businesses to run. It really shouldn't bother me. I'm turning twenty-three for Christ's sake. It's not like it's a big deal. I will be fine. If they all forgot, I'll take myself to the spa, get a massage, get my hair done. Whatever. I don't need to acknowledge another year of getting older anyway.

A pair of strong arms wraps around me from behind as I'm bending down counting bottles of vodka under the bar. I smile. I know who these arms belong to. Me, that's who. Standing up, I spin around and wrap my own arms around Dean's neck. Standing on my tiptoes, I smash my lips on his. He lifts me off the floor, sitting my ass on the bar top. I spread my legs open as far as they will go in this skirt, wrapping them around his waist, as he steps between them and claims my lips again.

"Mmm, have I told you how much I love working here?" I ask him between kisses.

"You're about to be fucking fired. Both of you!" Zac yells from behind me. I laugh, looking up at Dean. It's not the first time Zac has caught us like this. It won't be the last.

"Ella, get your ass off the bar. People eat off that. Dean, don't you have, I don't know, work to do?" Zac says.

"Nothing more important than what I'm doing right now." Dean winks at me. I melt into him.

"Okay, gross. That's still my fucking sister, asshole."

"Well, I actually do have work I have to get back to." I push on Dean's chest, and he steps back, allowing me to jump down. I bend back over and continue counting the bottles of vodka.

I hear Dean curse and groan behind me. "Don't you have staff to do stocktake for you? There is no reason why you need to be fucking bent over like that in that fucking skirt. Well, not at work at least."

"Fucker," Zac says as he throws a cushion at Dean's head. I look up just in time to see the cushion hit him straight between the eyes. "Next one's gonna be a fucking bullet," Zac grunts as he storms off.

Dean looks back at me. "Well, don't you have someone else to do that? Because if you don't, I can get one of the guys to come do it."

"No, I need to do it myself."

"Okay, well, I'm staying put right here until you're finished. I'll keep you company while you count."

"Suit yourself." I shrug as I bend back down under the bar.

"Fucking hell," Dean growls. I laugh.

As much as we have explored each other's bodies over the last two weeks—and it's been a lot—we still haven't had sex. He says that my first time needs to be special, that he wants to wait to make sure it's as special as what I deserve.

I'm getting tired of waiting. I want him, more than ever. I want to give him something of myself that no one else will ever get. I'm going through the million ways I can continue to torture him like I am now, bending over like this. I could definitely squat down, sit on the floor. But where would be the fun in that? Dean clears his throat.

"We have plans tonight, Princess. You're taking the night off," he then says out of nowhere.

"Uh, no, I'm not. I have work to do, Dean. I can't just take a night off. It doesn't work like that." I stand up and cross my arms over my chest.

"Well, I happen to be really good friends with the boss, and he agreed to give you the night off."

"Dean, you can't do that. You can't just tell me to jump and expect me to say how high."

"It's not like that, Princess. I have a surprise. I want to take you out somewhere nice before I give it to you." I squint at him. It's not that I don't trust him. I just know he's really fucking good with his words, and sometimes, what he says and what I hear are two completely different things.

"Why do I feel like you're hiding something?" I ask.

"Because I am, obviously. I just said I had a surprise for you. But you need to take the night off to get it."

"Okay, I'll take tonight off. But only tonight. Do not make this a regular thing, Dean. I want people to take me seriously at this job. They won't do that if I'm slacking off."

"Anyone that doesn't take you seriously can fuck off and work somewhere else. You were made for this job, Princess." He wraps his arms around me, pulling me in tight. I get lost in his scent, his touch, his everything.

"What do I need to wear to this thing?"

"What you've got on is good. I'll meet you in your office at six. Be ready to leave." He kisses my forehead before walking away. I watch his ass until he's out of sight around the corner. Damn, he's got a fine ass, especially in those grey dress pants.

I shake off the thoughts of stripping him out of those pants and having my way with him. I have work to do. And apparently, I have to do it faster, considering I won't be here tonight.

I'm starting to get anxious about what and where it is Dean's taking me. I've been pacing my office for the last ten minutes, trying to figure out what this surprise could be. I'm really fucking hoping we're finally going to have sex.

I didn't wait four years for him to decide he wants me, only to then be denied and told I have to wait longer. That's bullshit. I don't need some place fancy or candles lit everywhere. I don't need some grand romantic gesture. I just need him. Why can't he see that? Just him is what will make it special to me.

My door opens and Dean swaggers in. Yes, swaggers. He's still wearing those grey dress pants. Although, now he has on a matching jacket and a white business shirt with the top buttons undone, giving me just a peek of that delicious skin he's hiding underneath.

When I look at him like this, I can definitely see the refined McKinley bloodline. I don't know why I never saw it before, probably because I was focused on remembering the times I saw him shirtless, in nothing but a pair of workout shorts or sweatpants.

His muscles on full display, his skin would glisten with sweat as he worked out with Bray. I used to stare at the tattoos on his arms and shoulders. I would doodle drawings of the swirls in my notebooks. I'd pretend to be doing homework, while storing those images in my memory and keeping them for myself.

"If you keep looking at me like that, Princess, we won't make it out of this office." Dean grabs my hand and pulls me out the door.

"Well, that doesn't sound like a bad idea," I suggest. "Where did you say we were going anyway?"

Dean turns his head back to me and smirks. "I didn't."

I follow him out to his car and let him open my door. I sit down and buckle my seat belt. I really don't like surprises. It's unnerving.

Dean jumps in the driver's seat and pulls out of

the carpark. He reaches over and grabs my hand. I'm trying really hard not to freak out. I've been trying to be the normal Ella, the one whom everyone needs. But it's getting harder and harder. Like right now, not knowing where I'm going, what I'm going to be doing, it's killing me.

"I can hear you thinking, Princess. Talk to me. What's wrong?"

"Nothing," I lie.

"Don't lie to me, Ella. We are better than that. We are more than that. There is nothing you can't tell me." He brings my hand up to his mouth.

"Okay. Don't take this the wrong way. Because I love that you want to surprise me and all. But I kind of really don't like surprises. It's making me anxious, not knowing where I'm going, what I'll be doing. I can't shake this feeling of doom and gloom when I don't know. It makes my skin itch."

"Fuck. I'm sorry. I should have known. I'm really sorry. You've been stressing about this all day? Why the fuck didn't you come and tell me you needed to know more details? I never want to make you feel anxious," he rambles.

"I was trying not to be," I admit.

"Never try to be anything but yourself with me, Ella. You are the most perfect version of you."

"Okay."

"I mean it. All right, well, I may have planned a little get away. We're heading to the airport. We're getting on a jet. We're going away for two nights."

"What? Two nights? Dean, I can't be gone for two nights. I have work to do!"

"Well, that's not all of the surprise, Princess. I also have our entire family waiting for us on the plane. They're meant to jump out and yell surprise when you walk on. This is your birthday trip, Ella. Happy birthday, Princess."

"You remembered? I thought everyone forgot," I admit.

"I'd never forget the day that God created the most perfect fucking creature. My Princess." Dean looks across and winks at me.

"I'm not perfect, Dean. I'm nothing but a broken Princess. I couldn't even handle letting you surprise me for my birthday. What the fuck is wrong with me?"

"There is nothing wrong with you. Who the fuck cares if you need to know where we are going? That's not being broken, Ella. That's being cautious. And cautious is a character strength, not a weakness. You are not broken. I will keep telling you that until you believe it yourself. I don't care if I have to tell you for the rest of our lives."

"Thank you. This is going to be the best fucking birthday I've ever had. Because on this birthday, I get to wake up next to you. That's all I need. I don't need fancy grand gestures and gifts. Although I'm not saying no to gifts. Just so we're clear, gifts are most certainly welcome. But the best gift of all, I already have." I can't help but smile.

A few minutes pass, and we're almost at the

airport. It's killing me not knowing exactly where it is we are going. I don't want to ask. I trust Dean with every fibre of my being. Knowing my brothers are also waiting on the plane, I can breathe a little easier.

I'm just glad I thought to grab my laptop before leaving the club today. If Dean thinks I'm going to stop working for two solid days, he's dreaming. There is no way I can slack off now. I'm so close to figuring out the puzzle around Zac's accounts. I can feel it. I know whatever is happening is right in front of me. I just need to dig a little deeper to get to it.

Dean pulls into a little private airport. I've never been here before. He stops right alongside a small private jet. There's a red carpet that leads up to the stairs of the plane.

"Did you seriously hire a private jet, Dean? You know I'd be more than happy to fly commercial. This is too much."

"Ah, not exactly. I didn't hire it, Princess," he says as he looks out the window at the jet in question.

"Well, who did? Please tell me Zac did not do this. All I sent him for his birthday was a pair of socks." I really need to put more effort into my crappy gift giving.

"It wasn't Zac. I didn't hire the plane because I own it. Well, my family owns it." He's a little uncertain as he tells me this. I know his family's wealth is an issue for him. But a private jet. Damn.

"You've had your own jet this whole time?" I punch him in the arm. "You mean, every time we went on trips, I didn't have to sit in a commercial plane, next to smelly guys and screaming kids. Way to hold out on a girl, Dean!" I smile at him. I don't think I can hold in my excitement. I want to get on this plane already.

"Ella, everywhere you've been, you have flown first class. That's hardly roughing it, Princess. And the only smelly guys you've ever sat next to were your own brothers." He laughs.

"Yeah, but Bray!" I don't need to say anything else, just his name alone is an explanation.

"Don't worry, babe. I'll make sure you won't be sitting anywhere near him. Nobody should be put through the hell of sitting next to him on a flight. Ever."

I lean over, grab his face and kiss him. "In case I forget later, thank you for taking me on this trip. I've had the time of my life."

His face lights up as he smiles. I get lost in those eyes. They are so blue, like the ocean, the prettiest damn eyes I've ever seen.

"The fun's just beginning, Princess." Dean gets out and walks around to my door, opening it for me. I take hold of his hand and climb out of his car.

We walk, hand in hand, up the steps of the plane.

"Remember to act surprised," Dean whispers in my ear, just before we enter the doors.

As if on cue, everyone jumps out and screams, "Surprise!" Within seconds, I'm scooped up off the ground and spun around in circles by Bray. By the time he puts me down, I'm so dizzy I have to hold on to the wall next to me.

"Happy birthday, Lil Sis. How the hell are you twenty-three already? It seems like just yesterday you were in nappies?" Bray ruffles my hair, which lands him a punch to his stomach. To his credit, he at least pretends that my punch hurts.

"Oh fuck, Ella. What was that for?" He leans over, pretending to be winded.

I don't have time to answer him before Zac has me wrapped in his arms. I sink into him, burying my head in his chest. His chin rests on my head. There's something about Zac's hugs. They've always seemed like home to me.

"Happy birthday, Ella," Zac whispers as his hand runs down my hair. He's squeezing a little tighter than usual, and for a little longer. It's almost like he doesn't want to let go. I don't make a move. If he needs a moment, I'll give it to him.

"Thanks, Zac," I whisper back.

"Okay, move aside. Stop hogging her. She's my sister too," Reilly says while shoving Zac. She sends him a wink and a grin while she pries me out of his arms.

Zac clears his throat. I look up at him to see his eyes watering. This happens every birthday. Zac will go over the top on the gift giving, get emotional and clingy towards me. And then the next day, he goes back to the normal, brooding, grouchy Zac. I think occasions like this make him miss our parents more than usual. We all do.

"Happy birthday, Ella. I picked out your gift too, so if Bray tries to take credit, don't believe him," she says while hugging me. She lets go with a huge grin on her face. Looking over my shoulder towards Dean, she adds with a devilish smile, "I also packed for you. I went shopping and got you everything you could possibly need for this trip."

All three men groan at the same time. I laugh. They do not approve of Reilly's fashion choices. Well, Bray approves of them on her, just not on me. I personally love her taste. She has style. I do think she purposely chooses the most revealing outfits she can, just to get a rise out of the guys.

"What the fuck, Reilly? I thought Alyssa was doing the shopping. Princess, forget about leaving the hotel room if you don't have appropriate clothing. Actually, I'll just order you some new stuff," Dean says.

Bray punches Dean in the arm. "Ow, the fuck, Bray?" Dean curses.

"Don't yell at my wife." Bray smirks, then punches him again. "Also, my sister and a hotel room. No, just fucking no!" Bray says as he walks down the aisle of the plane.

"Sorry, Reilly, I shouldn't have yelled. But really? You couldn't let Alyssa shop?" Dean says with a pout.

"Sorry, I got caught up. Don't worry, I'm sure it's fine. Reilly also went shopping for me for this trip. I haven't even looked at what goodies she got me yet." Alyssa comes in to hug me with Ash in her arms.

"No! Fuck no, Sunshine. Whatever she bought you, it can be donated. Probably to the local strippers," Zac growls.

"Aunty El. It's your birthday," Ash says while reaching his arms out for me.

Taking him off Alyssa, I kiss all over his face. "It sure is, little guy."

"Do we get cake?" he asks, all serious.

"I hope so. What kind of birthday would it be without cake?" I ask.

"A yucky one," Ash replies, nodding his head.

"Okay, Ash, come on. We need to get you buckled in." Alyssa takes him back and walks down the aisle.

I look down the aisle, finally getting a chance to take in the room. There are luxury cream leather seats. Two sets of four seats face each other in the middle of the plane, while another set of seats sit behind them.

Bray and Reilly are getting the twins clipped into baby seats in one section, while Alyssa settles Ash into one on the other side. Zac sits, watching them intently with a whisky in his hand.

"Come on, I'll give you a little tour." Dean takes my hand, leading me down the aisle past the seating. He walks through a little doorway. Behind the wall is a small galley kitchen with staff busying around. Two blonde flight attendants look up the moment we walk through.

One plasters on a big fake smile while pushing her tits out. "Mr. McKinley. Welcome. Is there anything I can get you?" Her sickeningly sweet voice runs through me like nails on a chalkboard. Why do I have the sudden urge to claw her eyes out?

"Kristy, this is Ella. My girlfriend. Whatever she wants, make sure she gets it," Dean says, then he continues to pull me through to the other side of the kitchen. I don't miss the scowl "Kristy" sends me.

"Nice staff," I mumble once we're on the other side.

Dean looks down at my face, his eyes scrunched. Without warning, he bends and picks me up, throwing me over his shoulder.

"Ah, Dean. Put me down!" I squeal.

"Not a chance," he says as he opens another door. I can't see where we are, due to the fact that I'm upside down.

He shuts the door behind him and throws me down. I scream as I land on a mattress. I get a brief chance to look around before Dean's on top of me, caging me in.

We're in a bedroom. On a jet, in a bedroom! Seriously, this is another level of traveling.

"It's cute that you're jealous, Princess. But you have absolutely no reason to be," Dean says as he kisses up my neck.

My legs wrap around his waist. I lift my hips to grind my core along his hardening cock. "Mmm, I'm not jealous," I moan.

"Sure you're not. But if you were, you don't need to be. There is only one you. And you, Princess, are all I've ever needed. You are everything I could ever want, all wrapped up in a fucking beautiful package." He lifts his head to make eye contact with me.

"Always have. Always will," he says.

"Always have. Always will," I repeat our little declaration.

Dean jumps up. "Okay, we need to go get seated. We're taking off in less than five minutes." He holds his hand out for me.

I groan. "I'd much prefer to stay in here," I grumble.

"Yeah. And I prefer to stay alive. You moaning out loud back here, that's one sure way to have Zac pulling the fucking trigger."

Taking his hand, I ask, "What's up with him today? He seems off?"

"Not sure." He shrugs.

"Okay. Let's go sit with the riffraff, shall we?"

Dean laughs. "That riffraff is our family."

Chapter Twelve

Dean

"I'M JUST GOING to sit with Alyssa for a bit." Ella turns to me just before we make it back out to the main area of the jet.

"Okay. Do you want anything to drink? Eat?" We're back in the galley with the overly friendly stewardess. Ella looks over at the two women, then shakes her head. "No, I'm good," she whispers and walks out the door.

"I need a bottle of Cristal and six glasses," I tell Kristy and Chantel. Before I walk out, I add, "Chantel, I want you to serve us throughout the flight. Kristy, you can keep yourself busy back here, I'm sure."

Chantel nods. "Of course, Sir," she says while busying herself pulling out champagne flutes and placing them on a tray.

When I walk out, I see Zac is sitting on a seat behind the two sets of sofas. Ella is sitting across from Alyssa and Ash, smiling and chatting with Ash.

Looking across, I can see Bray is about to lose it. For someone who can hop in a cage with any opponent without a trace of fear, he's a fucking pussy when it comes to flying. He catches my eye. Great, I knew better than to make eye contact.

"Dean, how many times did you say the pilots did the pre-flight check again?" he asks.

"I didn't."

"But they did more than one check, right? You know what, maybe we should stay behind. You know, take care of shit here." He's about to unbuckle his belt, which is done up hilariously tight around his waist, when Reilly interjects.

"Babe, calm down. If you get off this plane, you're going alone. The girls and I are going on this trip," she says.

"Fuck, Reilly, we can have our own little staycay here. We don't need to be in a death trap millions of miles in the damn air." I can see the sweat run down his face. He really doesn't like flying.

"We're taking off. It's too late to get off the plane, Bro." I smirk at him.

"Bray, it's fine. It's a short flight. You will survive," Reilly says. "Here, make sure Lily drinks this as we're going up." Reilly shoves a pink sippy cup with water in it at him.

I take a seat next to Zac and settle in. I'd much

rather be sitting next to my girl. But at least I can try to figure out what's crawled up Zac's ass today.

"What's up?" I ask.

"We're about to be," he says and laughs at his own bad joke.

"You should save the bad dad jokes for Bray; he's better at them," I say.

"Probably."

"Okay, chatty Kathy. No need to talk my fucking ear off," I retort, my voice dripping with sarcasm.

Zac breathes in heavily and sighs. He looks over my head to Alyssa and Ella, both now playing with Ash.

"Not here," he says, then nods his head towards the back of the plane.

"Let's go." I get up and lead him towards the bedroom in the back. Once inside, he takes one look at the ruffled bedding.

"Nope, no. Fucking hell. I'm not sitting in a room where you just had my sister on that bed." He scowls.

"Grow up. We were in here for two minutes, asshole."

"Nope, a lot can happen in two minutes," he says.

I scrunch my nose at him. "For you, maybe."

He just stares at me, his face stone hard.

"I haven't slept with her, you know. Your sister is still very much intact." I tell him. Not really sure why, but hopefully it puts his mind at ease.

He tilts his head at me. "She's still a virgin?" he asks.

I nod. "For now."

"Fucker!" he growls, then breathes out through his teeth. "Okay, have you suddenly found Jesus? Waiting for marriage? Cause I can get on board with that." He smiles.

"I think it's a bit fucking late for Jesus. *For both of us.* Now, tell me what the fuck is going on with you."

Zac sits on the edge of the bed, running his hands through his hair.

"I received an email today," he says.

"Okay, I'm sure you get plenty of emails every day. What was special about this one?" I lean against the wall, crossing my legs out in front of me.

"Here, look for yourself," he says as he hands me his phone. "I got this about ten minutes before you guys got here."

I take his phone and look at the screen. I scroll up and down the email a few times, not believing what I'm seeing, what I'm reading. This has to be some sort of sick joke. It can't be real.

"What? Who? What the fuck is this?" I ask, my shaking hands gripping the phone. I look at the door. I should be out there. I need to be out there. I'm about to go back out when Zac stops me.

"Wait. Dean. You can't go out there like this. They will all know something's wrong."

"Something *is* fucking wrong, Zac. *That* is fucking wrong," I say, pointing to the phone.

"You think I don't know that?" he shouts. "Fuck!"

"I'm not leaving her side. From now on, where she

goes, I go. I will not let anyone get to her, Zac. I just got her back." I'm not sure if I'm trying to convince him or myself.

"We all just got her back. We can't tell her about this, Dean. I don't know if she can handle it," he says.

"That's not fair. We can't keep this from her. She shouldn't be expected to be blind to this. And I'm not about to lie to her."

"Okay. But let's wait until after the weekend. I don't want to ruin her birthday."

I agree. I won't let anything ruin her weekend. "Fine. But I'm putting a team on this now," I assert, pulling out my phone. I need to know who the fuck sent that email.

"I've already got external friends working on it. No one from the club can know about this. We don't know who it is, but it is someone from the inside."

"Who's working on it?"

"A hacker friend." Zac's being purposefully evasive with his answer.

"You don't have any friends. Other than me," I counter.

"You're right. But, in this case, this friend, she is doing me a favour."

I can't just sit around and do nothing. And he can't expect me to sit around and do nothing after seeing that email.

"Well, she had better be fucking good. I want to know who the fuck thinks they can threaten Ella and live to see the next day!"

My mind replays the images of the email, over and over on a loop. There were three photos. All of Ella. One of her in her office. One at the gym. One at her apartment. All times when she's been alone. But the cryptic message that accompanied the pictures, that's what's most disturbing.

People who look too hard don't see what's coming.

There is not a doubt in my mind that that message is a direct threat to Ella. I need to get back out to her. I need to have my eyes on her.

The rest of the flight was uneventful, apart from Bray having a major fucking panic attack about the landing. The fucker actually prayed a Hail Mary. It shocked me that he even knew the prayer. Although, I don't think he could say enough of them to save his soul. After the shit we've done in our lives, I know where I'm going, and I'm fine with that.

Ella is craning her neck to see out of the car windows, trying to take in all the scenery. I think it all looks the same. Palm trees and beaches, there's not much more.

We're on our way to the boat terminal, where we will be getting on a ferry to the island resort I've booked. She still doesn't know where we are, or where we are heading. I know it's got to be killing her, the not knowing. Yet, she hasn't asked.

"You still like the beach, right?" I ask.

"What kind of person doesn't like the beach, Dean?" she throws back at me.

"An idiot?" I question. Personally, I'm not a fan. But I know she loved the beaches in Hawaii. I couldn't make that possible for a two-day trip. So, I picked the next best thing, the tropics of North Queensland.

"Yes, only a fucking idiot would hate the beach." She smirks at me, knowing full well I don't like it.

"Well, it's a good thing you love it. Because we are heading to Green Island. We're going to be stuck on the beach for the next two days, Princess." I try my hardest to hide my disgust. This is for Ella. Her happiness is my happiness.

"Wait, where are we?" she asks excitedly.

"We're in Cairns. The island we're going to is about a forty-five minute boat ride from the mainland. It's small. I booked the whole resort out, so it's just us. And it's on the Great Barrier Reef."

The squeal she lets out is enough to deafen the whole damn country. She's jumping up and down in her seat like a kid on Christmas. I guess I picked the right place.

"Oh my god! Dean! The Great Barrier Reef! Are you serious? Do you know how long I've wanted to come here? Fuck, I can't wait. Oh my god! I fucking love you!" she screams.

Her excitement is contagious. I fucking love it. I can't help but smile and be excited with her. "I fucking love you too, Princess." I smash our lips together, our tongues entwined.

I'm just about to unplug her belt and pull her on top of me when the car comes to a stop. She groans when I pull back, her kiss-swollen lips looking so fucking inviting. I want nothing more than to slide my cock between those lips.

I have to adjust myself before stepping out of the car. I've been waiting to take things further with Ella. Much to her disagreement, I want us to take things slow in the bedroom. We've done plenty, don't get me wrong. I make sure she comes more times a day than she can count. But we haven't had sex.

I told her it's because I want to make it special. It's her first time. She deserves romance, candles, flowers, all that crap. But really, it's because I don't want to hurt her. And I know it's going to hurt. I know she has a strained relationship with pain. How will she react to that kind of pain? Is it going to set her back in her progress? I have no fucking idea what I'm doing.

What I do know is that I need to man up and put us all out of our misery. Her, me, and my fucking blue balls. When I step out of the car, the humidity hits me like a fucking freight train.

Sweat instantly starts to drip from my head. It's six o'clock at night and it's this fucking hot. How am I going to handle the day hours? How do people live in this shit?

I help Ella out of the car and we walk hand in hand to the rest of the bunch, who are already waiting. Bray has both twins in his arms, one on each hip. Reilly looks flustered and is busy doing some shit to her hair. Zac stands there with a scowl on his face, Ash sitting up on his shoulders. Alyssa's holding his hand and arm like she's trying to hold him back.

"What the fuck took you so long?" Bray asks. He looks at Ella then adds, "Actually, don't bloody answer that. I don't want to know."

"Bray, I swear if he starts copying those words of yours, you will pay," Alyssa scolds him while pointing to Ash.

"Uncle Bray said bad words," Ash says.

"Uncle Bray is allowed. When you're big, you'll be allowed to, too, mate," Bray says to Ash.

"I'm nearly four. I am big now," Ash says.

"Huh, four. No way! I thought you were at least twenty," Bray says with his most serious voice.

"Did you really have to pick somewhere so humid? My hair will not cope with this heat, Dean," Reilly complains.

"Yes, I did. Ella likes the beach." I shrug.

"You know what else Ella is going to like?" Reilly asks me with a devious smirk.

I don't want to know what she's going to say. But I can't fucking help myself. I play into her bait. "What?"

"Those little string bikinis I got her." Reilly smiles.

"Burn them," Zac says to me.

I don't get time to reply as we're greeted by the ferry staff.

"McKinley Party?" a young guy in a tank and board shorts asks while staring at Ella.

"That's us," I say while pulling Ella in close and kissing her forehead. The fucker looks away. That's right. She's mine.

"Right, we're ready to board," he says, then turns, leading the way to the ferry.

"Way to mark your territory, Bro," Bray remarks with a laugh.

"Shut up, idiot!" Ella steps up to him and takes one of the twins. Don't ask me which one it is. I still can't fucking tell. Everyone else seems to know though.

"We're going on a boat, Lily," Ella coos. "I can't wait to get there." She smiles at me.

The sight of Ella with a baby on her hip shouldn't look so damn good. But damn, do I want to make her the mother of my children. One day. Right now, I'm happy having her all to myself.

We all follow the douche onto the ferry, and settle in for the forty-five minute boat ride. It's so fucking hot. I take my shirt off, before using it to wipe the sweat from my face. Ella is sitting there playing with Lily and Hope. She looks up at me, and her eyes widen.

"Ah, Reilly?" she asks, not breaking her stare from me.

Reilly laughs. "What's up?"

"Take the girls back. I'm going to go get a drink from the bar. Anyone want anything?" she asks.

She doesn't wait for an answer. "Dean, you can help me." She pulls my hand, dragging me behind her through the boat. She gets to a bathroom door, looks around, then pulls me through it before shutting and locking it behind us.

Before I know it, she jumps up, wraps her legs around my waist and clings to me like a damn spider monkey. My hands instinctively go to her ass, holding her weight up easily.

Her lips find mine; her tongue pushes through, seeking mine. Her pussy grinds on my cock. Spinning us around, I pin her back against the wall. I groan out loud. I want her so fucking bad. My cock is fucking aching. My hands slide under the fabric of her skirt, landing on her bare ass. My hands squeeze the fleshy globes so hard, I won't be surprised if she ends up with my fingerprints marking her.

Her moans of pleasure echo in the small room. The only thing between us are my shorts and the thin lace of her thong.

"Dean, I need…" Her words trail off.

"What do you need, Princess?" I ask while grinding into her core, dry humping her like a fucking teenager.

"More, I need more!" she moans out.

Picking her up higher, I sit her thighs on my shoulders. Her hands go to my head to help her balance. My face now buried in her sweet pussy, my tongue runs along her lips and over the lace of her already wet panties. I can taste her through the lace. It's intoxicating. I want to drown in her.

Her thighs tighten around my neck, trapping my head. Her fingers pull at the strands of my hair. Then she's screaming my name. Fuck, I love hearing her scream out my name like this.

Chapter Thirteen

Ella

"OH MY GOSH, Dean, this place is amazing. I can't believe you did all this. *For me.*" I spin around taking in the opulence of the room. There's a four-poster bed. A huge four-poster bed with white netting draped down the sides and white bedding.

There's rose petals over the bed, with the words "Happy birthday, Princess" spelled out. The room is filled with natural wood décor and beachy tones. The blue sofa is covered with white and blue cushions. Shells decorate the coffee table in front of it.

Sheer white curtains hang from the large sliding glass doors that overlook the ocean. We are literally on the beach. The sound of the waves crashing fills the room.

There's a bottle of champagne on the bench with

two glasses next to it. *That* needs to be opened sooner rather than later.

"It's so beautiful, Dean. I don't know what to say."

"You don't need to say anything, Princess. I'm glad you like the place." Huh. He seems a little off. I've noticed since he came out of the room with Zac, he's been a little weird. I didn't want to bring it up. But I really can't read him at the moment.

"Are you okay? I know you don't really like the beach. So, you know, if you want to head back to the mainland, we can. I don't mind."

"We're not leaving here, babe. I'm good. I promise. Now, let's pop this bottle and get the celebration started." He heads over to the champagne and pours us each a glass.

"Mmm." I moan at the taste of the sweet bubbly goodness on my tongue.

"Fuck, Ella! If you keep moaning like that, we won't be leaving this room."

"I'm good with that," I say with a shrug as I jump onto the middle of the bed.

"No. We have dinner reservations with everyone. In twenty minutes. Your bags should be in the closet already," he says, looking towards the closet.

When I don't make an effort to leave the bed, he groans, "Come on, Princess. Don't make this harder than it already is for me." His eyes avert down as he adjusts his cock in his pants. I can't help but lick my lips at the sight. His shorts are doing nothing to hide his hardness. "Oh fuck, don't do that! Let's just get dinner done. We'll be back here before you know it," he begs.

I laugh. "Okay. But just so you know, I would have preferred to have you for dinner." I wink as I walk past him towards the closet. I hear him curse under his breath.

Digging through the suitcase Reilly packed me, I'm giddy like a kid on Christmas. God, she's a good shopper. I choose a sheer Camilla halter dress. I pick out a black strapless bikini to wear under it. Taking my goodies, I walk into the bathroom for a quick shower and to get changed.

"I'll be five minutes, then the bathroom is all yours." I kiss Dean on the cheek as I pass.

"You know we can save time, and water, if we shower together."

I consider his offer briefly. "If I get you naked in that shower right now, we most certainly won't make dinner," I say.

"Good point."

I shower in less than five minutes. leaving my hair hanging wet down my back. I'm sure, in this heat, it won't take long to dry anyway. The dress Reilly picked out, is more sheer than I thought. You can clearly see my bikini underneath it. I love it. I throw on the hotel robe. I'll wait until we're walking out the door before I drop this outfit on Dean.

I wait while Dean showers and gets dressed. It's bloody torture, knowing just what his body looks like with water dripping down it. I close my eyes and envision his rock-hard abs, suds running down them and leading to his hard cock. I can almost feel the girth of it in my hands. Mmm, maybe I should have taken him up on that offer to shower together.

"Good thoughts?" Dean's voice makes me jump out of the chair.

"Jesus! Warn a girl next time," I shriek with my hand on my chest.

Dean tilts his head. His eyes rove up and down my body. My cheeks heat at the thought of being caught daydreaming about his cock.

"Sorry, what were you thinking about just now?" He smirks.

"Uh, how great it's going to be to get in the ocean tomorrow."

"Sure you were." He winks. "We should get going." He heads to the door. When his back turns, I take the robe off and throw it on the bed. He doesn't look back up until he's holding the door open for me.

"Oh, hell no!" he growls, the sound momentarily stopping me in my tracks.

"What's wrong?" I ask, trying to use the most innocent voice I can muster.

"What's wrong? What's wrong, she asks! Did you forget something? You know, like the rest of your fucking clothes?" He shakes his head.

I walk out the door before he gets a chance to lock us in.

"No, I didn't forget anything. Why? Do I not look good in this dress?" I ask on the other side of the door, taking small backwards steps while picking at the fabric. His steps follow me.

"That's not the problem. You are fucking gorgeous! The problem is that's a... I don't know what that is. But I do know dresses are meant to cover your body. That does not hide a damn thing."

"Well, I like it. Remind me to thank Reilly when I see her," I say as I turn around.

"I'm going to fucking kill..." His voice trails off. I turn to look over my shoulder at him. He's stopped, his eyes wide, and staring directly at my ass.

"Jesus fucking Christ. Ella, I can see your ass," Dean complains.

"I thought you said and I quote: *Princess, you have the best fucking ass I've ever seen.* What's wrong with it now?"

"Nothing's wrong with it! Your panties are not covering it is what's wrong. Every man and his dog are going to be ogling that fine fucking ass. I'm going to have to bury bodies. My weekend is going to be spent burying fucking bodies. Do you know how hard it is to dig six feet down *in sand*?" he asks, all serious.

"I thought you said we had this resort to ourselves. No one else is here, Dean. I hardly think Zac and Bray are going to be checking out my ass. Relax. Come on. We're already late."

"Fuck. There is staff here too, Ella," Dean says as he wraps his arm around my shoulder.

"Don't worry, babe. I'm sure Bray will be your muscle if you have to bury anyone." I shrug.

"Do you know how much that fucker complains about digging?" he asks. For a second, I actually think he's serious. He sounds serious. But he has to be joking. I know my brothers have done some shady dealings in the past. But burying bodies seems extreme.

I shake the thoughts off as we enter a gazebo. Fairy lights cover the roof. Our entire family is already sitting at the table chatting. The table is gorgeous. A white linen table cloth covers it with a blue runner down the middle. Candles are scattered around the table.

Dean stands behind me, his hands on my hips keeping me in place.

"You're late," Zac states, glaring at Dean.

"We wouldn't be if Reilly knew what was classified as a dress," Dean says.

"What?" Bray asks, confused.

"Oh, your extremely helpful wife bought this… whatever this is," Dean says, pointing to my dress.

I roll my eyes.

"It looks great! I love it," Reilly says.

"You look beautiful, Ella. Don't listen to the grouch," Alyssa adds.

"Thank you. He's overreacting," I tell Bray and Zac.

"Overreacting? Really. Okay. Princess, can I have this dance?" Dean steps in front of me, holding his hand out.

I'm confused. What's he up to? His eyes spark

with mischief. But I'm hardly going to pass up an opportunity to dance. I take his hand, and he twirls me around. I hear him count to three under his breath. Then I hear Zac.

"Ella, what the fuck?! Where are your fucking clothes?" he yells.

Dean pulls me against his chest, whispering in my ear, "Still think I'm overreacting?" He smirks as he leads me over to the chair and pulls it out for me.

"Babe, I love you. You're fucking perfect. But you're never shopping for my sister again!" Bray says to Reilly.

"Leave her alone. I love the stuff she got me. Thank you, Reilly."

"You're welcome." She winks at me. All three of us girls laugh. At the same time, the men at the table groan.

Dinner was great. I'm stuffed. We had a variety of deliciously fresh seafood and salads. Thankfully, Bray and Zac had to get the kids to bed, which means we got out of there early. I'm eager to get back to the room. I want Dean so bad right now. Is tonight the night? I feel like I've been waiting for this night forever.

As soon as we're through the door of our room, I pull the dress up over my head. I turn around and face Dean as I reach behind myself and unclip my bikini top. Walking backwards towards the bed, I pull my bikini bottoms down my legs and kick them off to the side.

"Dean, if I asked for something for my birthday, would you be able to give it to me?" I ask as I climb up on the bed and sit on my knees. I spread my legs, keeping them open. His eyes roam all over my body.

Shivers run up and down my spine, my skin tingling, burning, with his gaze. My own hands begin to travel up and down my thighs.

"Princess. I can get you anything you want. You know that. Money is not an object. What is it that you want?" he asks as he licks his lips. He still hasn't moved. He's standing in front of the closed door.

"What I want won't cost money," I say as my hands travel up the sides of my waist, his eyes following their movement. "I want you to make love to me, Dean. Now. Right here. I don't want to wait anymore."

He's at the side of the bed before I can even blink, his hands in my hair. He tilts my head up. Looking into my eyes, he asks, "Are you sure?"

"Yes. One hundred percent."

"Okay," he says as he pulls his shirt over his head.

I reach up and unbutton his shorts. I've been

waiting all day to get my hands on his cock. I need it. *Now*. My hands are shoved away as he pulls his shorts down his legs.

Dean climbs on top of me, pushing me back onto the bed. My legs wrap around his waist. I can feel his hardness at my centre. I rub my clit along his cock.

Dean's hand comes around my throat. He doesn't squeeze, just holds my head still. "I love you so fucking much, Ella Williamson," he says before slamming his lips onto mine. His hand leaves my throat and travels down, between our bodies and right to my clit, where his fingers rub in slow, torturous circles.

I'm going crazy with need. I can feel my vagina pulsing, searching for something. Dean inserts two fingers. I feel so full... I wonder if his cock is even going to fit inside me. The thought does not stay long as pleasure ripples through me.

"I need you inside me now, Dean," I groan. His fingers feel great, but they're not what I want right now.

Dean pulls his fingers out. I can feel him line the head of his cock up with my entrance. He stops kissing me as he stares down at me, his cock slowly creeping into my core. *Inch by inch*. I'm stretched, so fucking full.

It hurts, slightly. But I like it. I want him to stretch me out. He gently pulls back and slides back in, with just the tip. Not all the way. I'm so wet, I can feel my own juices dripping.

"Tell me if it hurts too much. If the pain is too

much, I'll stop. Promise me, Ella, that you'll tell me to stop if you need me to?" His voice is so strained. Is that what's been holding him back? He's worried about hurting me. I'm not afraid of the pain.

But that's the problem. He's not afraid of me hurting. He's afraid of me liking the pain too much. I can't guarantee that I won't. But I can give him the promise he needs. "I promise I'll tell you if I need you to stop."

Dean buries his cock all the way, in one thrust, ripping right through the barrier. A searing pain tears through me. It's wrong how good I feel right now. I embrace the pain. I let it wash over me. Dean holds still inside me. My pussy convulses around him. I try to fight the pleasure. It's wrong. I shouldn't feel this good right now. I try to fight the fog that washes over me, but it feels so good. I grind my clit against his pelvis and it sends me over the edge into pure bliss.

An orgasm takes over as I scream his name. My whole body shakes with intense pleasure. Dean stays still, buried inside of me. When I open my eyes, he's staring down at me. "Fuck, Ella! I fucking love watching you fall apart. We're going to talk about what just happened later. Right now, I need to start moving. You good?" he asks, not breaking eye contact.

"Mmhmm, better than good." I smile, probably looking like the lovesick fool I am. The lovesick fool who's no longer a virgin. Dean leans down and kisses up the side of my neck, nibbling on the lobe of my right ear as he begins to slowly thrust in and out of me.

"Fucking hell. You feel so goddamn good, Princess. I want to live inside your pussy. I want to stay cocooned in here forever." He pants as he begins to pick up his pace.

My legs are tightly wrapped around his waist, my hips meeting his thrusts. "Oh Fuck!" I scream. I'm chasing that oblivion again. I'm so close. I need it, like I need my next breath. No matter how close I get, I can't reach it.

Dean sits back on his haunches, lifting both my legs into the air. My ankles rest on his shoulders as his hands dig into my hips, holding me up off the bed. He slams his cock all the way in, hitting an all new spot. What the fuck was that?

"Yes, that. Do that again," I demand.

"As you wish," Dean says as he starts to fuck me harder. Gone is the idea of making love. I want him to fuck me as hard as he can. With each thrust, I can feel euphoria getting closer and closer. I don't know what's wrong with me. Maybe I'm a one and done girl. Fuck that. I know I can get there again.

"Dean, I need…" I trail off not sure how to tell him.

"What do you need, Ella?" he asks, slowing his pace.

I shake my head no. I can't tell him. I can't let him see how messed up I am. "Nothing," I lie. "Keep going."

I can feel his intense stare on me. I can't look him in the eye. I don't want him to see that I can't find my orgasm again. That it's pissing me off. That I want him to hurt me so that I can get there.

Then he starts fucking me hard again. He turns his head and clamps his teeth down onto my left ankle. "Ah fuck. Yes!" *That.* That's what I need. My eyes roll back at the pleasure coursing through my body. I can feel my core quiver and tighten.

Dean bites my ankle again, in a new spot, the pain pushing me over the edge. My orgasm comes out of its hiding spot and hits me head-on. My body seizes up. I'm screaming, but I don't think any coherent words are coming out.

"Fuck!" Dean growls. I can feel his cock harden even more before I feel spurts of warm liquid inside me. He pumps a few more times with a mixture of curses and my name spilling from his mouth.

He lets my legs drop to the mattress and catches himself as he falls on top of me. I groan as he slides his cock out of me and lies down beside me. He pulls me into his arms, my head resting on his sweaty chest. I can feel the rapid beat of his pulse.

"Is it always like that?" I ask.

"No," he says without further explanation.

Was it bad for him? He came, so it couldn't have been that bad. But what if I did it wrong? Should I have done something else?

"Did you... Did you not like it?" I ask timidly.

Dean picks me up from under my arms, draping

my whole body over top of his. My legs straddle his waist. I can feel the mixture of our fluids seeping out of me. I go to move off him. I'm just going to make him messy.

"Don't move," Dean says, holding me tighter. "Look at me, Ella."

I look up, my nerves going haywire.

"I fucking loved every minute of it. Don't ever question if I like fucking you. I don't just like it. I love it. I said no because it's never been like that before. It's never been that good before. It's different with you, because I fucking love you, Ella. Always have. Always will." He brings my face to meet his as he kisses me ever so gently.

"So, can we do that again? Because I'm a fan," I ask.

Chapter Fourteen

Dean

THE SUN SHINES on my face. I can feel the coolness of the sea breeze sweep over me. I roll over, reaching out for Ella. It's odd that she's not already locked in under my arms. I've gotten used to waking up with her body thrown all over mine.

My arm reaches out and finds nothing but air, my hand slapping down on the empty spot where her body should be. The sheet's cold… She's been gone for a while. Then it hits me. She's gone. She's not there. She should be there.

I jump up and look around the quiet room. "Ella!" I call out. She's probably in the bathroom. Opening the bathroom door, all I see is the remnants of our mess from the night before. After we… well, I'd like to be a gentleman and say we made love, but what we did was fuck. After that, we sat in a bubble bath together until the water went cold. Bubbles and water ended up all over the place.

The realisation that she's not in the room sets in. My pulse quickens as panic takes over. Grabbing my phone, I hit her number. Come on, Princess, pick up the phone. The call rings out. Fuck!

I need to calm down, she's probably with one of her brothers. I dial Zac. *Come on, pick up, fucker.*

"What?" he asks grumbly. Fuck, he's still asleep, which means he's not with Ella.

"Is Ella with you?" I ask, trying my best not to let the panic run through my voice. The last thing I need is Zac tearing the place apart in his search for her.

I hear movement. "No, she's not. I'm up. I'll see you in two. She's probably just gone to the gym. Meet me there." How the fuck has he become the voice of reason?

"Okay, yeah. I'll meet you there," I stumble out.

"Dean. Calm the fuck down. We're on a deserted fucking island. Like I said, she's more than likely at the gym."

"Yeah. I know. It's just…" I let my sentence drift off.

"I know," he says before hanging up.

On my way to the gym — I know I shouldn't but I can't help myself — I call Bray. If Ella is at the gym, she'd likely meet up with him there. She likes to think she can kick his ass. I know for a fact that he lets her win every time she does.

Don't get me wrong, if she catches you off guard,

she'll get you down. Fuck, she did it to me, and I'm fucking six foot two. The girl can fight. She shouldn't ever have to, though.

The phone rings once before he picks up. Bray's always been the early riser type. "Yeah?" he answers.

"Is Ella with you?" I say, while running over to the gym.

"No, why? She get sick of your ass already?" he asks.

"I woke up and she wasn't in the room."

"Where are you?" he asks.

"Heading to the gym, to see if she's there." I'm just pushing through the gym doors when I come face to face with Bray.

We hang up the phones.

"She's not here," he says, while staring at me. *Reading me.* I turn around at the sound of Zac opening the door.

"She's not here," I say.

"Yeah, I gathered that," he replies. "Okay, Bray, go check the pool. We'll head down to the beach and look there."

"Ah, what the fuck is going on?" Bray asks. "Why are you all bent out of shape because Ella's not in your shadow?"

"Just find her. I'll explain later," Zac says, as he turns and walks out the door.

"What did you get up to last night?" Zac asks as we walk to the beach.

My eyes widen; my eyebrows go up to my hairline.

There is no fucking way I'm telling him what we did last night. I'm not that fucking stupid. I don't have to, though. By the look on my face, he already knows.

"Fucker! Don't you dare fucking say a thing," he says. I don't miss his hands twitching, opening and closing into fists by his sides. He wants to hit me. I'm surprised he's holding back.

"Wasn't planning on it, Bro." I smirk.

Once we're on the beach, we head back towards the portion alongside my and Ella's room.

There's not a soul out here. We're nearing the room when I see her. Everything inside me settles instantly. She's okay. She's walking out of the water.

"There she is." I point to the water. "Ella!" I yell out, getting her attention. She turns and waves at us.

"Fucking Reilly," Zac curses. For a moment, I don't understand what he's talking about. My eyes are too busy taking in the sight of Ella.

Then I get it—Ella, walking up out of the water, her dark hair wet down her back. She's wearing a white string bikini, the white contrasting against her olive complexion. Fuck me. She's fucking gorgeous, all curves in all the right places. Her breasts bounce as she picks up her speed, heading towards us. They look like they're in danger of falling out of the tiny bit of fabric, which is doing a shitty ass job of covering them.

Fuck, I have to adjust myself in my shorts. Zac lifts his shirt over his head and steps in front of me just before Ella reaches us. Before either of us knows what is happening, Zac's got his shirt over the top of Ella's head, covering her body from anyone's view.

Ella immediately pulls the shirt back over her head. "What the fuck, Zac?" she asks him, holding his now wet, scrunched-up shirt in her fisted hands.

"You obviously forgot your clothes when you left your room this morning. I thought I'd give you mine." He shrugs.

Ella slams the shirt into his chest. "You might want to reconsider taking your shirt off in public these days, old man," she says.

Zac's eyebrows draw down as he asks, "Why's that?"

Ella lets go of the shirt; it drops to the sand. She points up and down his body as she says, "Well, you know, that whole dad bod thing you have going on now."

The look on Zac's face is fucking gold. He looks down, rubbing a hand over his chest and abs. The man is as vain as they bloody come. Ella knew exactly how to hit him where it hurts. He's speechless as he picks up his shirt and shakes the sand out of it. Me? I'm busy laughing my ass off at him.

"Okay, well, I'll catch you both later," she says as she turns and starts walking the other way. My laughter dies really fucking quick when I see the view Ella is giving. The full view of her uncovered ass. She's wearing a fucking G-string bikini. I'm going to have Reilly banned from every damn store in Sydney.

I pull my own shirt over my head and throw it to

the side. "Ah, I'll catch you later, man," I mumble to Zac as I run and pick Ella up around the waist from behind. She lets out a mixture of squeals and curses as I run into the waves. Ever tried running with a hard cock? It's not bloody fun. I don't even like the fucking ocean. But it was either run into the ocean, or risk letting my best mate notice the raging hard-on I have for his sister.

Once I'm waist-deep in the water, I let Ella go. Throwing her a little, I watch as she goes under the water. Coming back up, she gasps as she wipes the water from her face and attempts to push her wet hair back.

She looks at me with murder in her eyes. It's a little scary how I've seen that exact expression on her brother, right before he actually killed someone.

"Morning, Princess." I smirk as I wrap my arms around her. Her body floats into mine, her legs wrapping around my waist. She doesn't get time to answer before my lips are connected with hers.

She opens for me instantly, our tongues duelling. The salty taste of the ocean water is strong on her lips. Her legs tighten, and she grinds her pussy against my hard cock. "Mmm, goddamn," I growl as I hold her ass still, cradling her pushed up against me.

Ella lays a trail of kisses up my neck, then stops to nibble on my earlobe. Fuck me! That feels good. "Babe, if you keep that up, I will fuck you right here, in the middle of the beach for everyone to see."

She blows on my ear gently, sending goosebumps

along my arms. "That sounds like a great idea. Let's do that after…" Her whispered words trail off.

"After what?" I ask.

"This!" she shrieks, before she spins herself around my body. I don't know how she does it, but she ends up on my fucking shoulders. The unexpected movement causes me to lose balance. I go head first into the water. When I come up, the sight that greets me steals my breath away.

Ella is standing, what she probably thinks is a safe distance, away. Her face is lit up with a huge fucking smile. She's laughing, albeit, at my expense. I'd let her dunk me every day if it meant having her this happy. She cups her hands and starts splashing water in my direction, still laughing. She seems so carefree in this moment.

It dawns on me that this, right here, is the most carefree I've seen her since she's come home. I make a note to make sure she has more experiences where she can just be herself — the beautiful, young woman with a heart of gold.

I'm in awe of her every single day and I don't even think she knows it. Ella stops splashing when she notices I haven't moved. I've been struck still with the breathtaking view of her. She starts floating closer to me.

"What's wrong?" Concern is written all over her features. And I'm the fucking asshole who just stole her happiness. *Again.* I'm starting to think that I'm too toxic for her. I've always known she's too good for me.

Unfortunately for her though, I'm a fucking selfish bastard and I have no plans of letting her go. Ever.

"Nothing's wrong." I smile. "I was just caught up in your beauty. It's been a while since I've seen you so happy and carefree." She's within my reach now. I grab her around the waist and pull her so her body is flush with mine. "I like it. I love seeing you smile, hearing you laugh. It's like everything is right in my world when you're happy."

Ella sighs and melts into me. "What's not to be happy about? I have everything I've ever wanted right here in my arms." She smiles up at me.

"Oh yeah? What's that?" I ask.

"Well, there's the ocean. And not just any ocean. We are literally in the Great Barrier Reef, Dean!" She looks up at the sky, letting her head fall back, her dark locks floating on the water. She picks her head up. "I am happy, Dean. With you, I'm happy. Don't ever doubt that. I can't promise that I won't have times of…" She doesn't finish the sentence. She doesn't need to.

"Princess, I need you to promise me something."

"What?"

"If you ever feel the urge to cut… If you ever get to that place, I want you to find me. Just find me. Please." I can't fathom the thought of her being alone and in that mindset. It scares the shit out of me… what could happen… what could go wrong.

"I promise I will try," she says. It's all I can ask, really. It's not like I'll be leaving her side until I find the fucker who sent that email to Zac anyway, which reminds me how I ended up on the beach so damn early in the morning.

"I need one more promise, babe. I need you to not leave the room without waking me again. When I woke up and you weren't there, I panicked. I don't like not knowing if you're safe. I don't ever want to relive those feelings."

"I'm sorry. You looked so peaceful sleeping. I didn't want to disturb you. And in case you've forgotten, there's no one else here. Look around. What could possibly happen to me here?"

"A lot," I grumble.

"Okay, well, I will do my best to wake you up. But if you end up with bags under your eyes because you lose beauty sleep, don't come blaming me."

I laugh. "Nice try. But I'm not as vain as your brothers, babe."

"How quickly do you think Zac ran to the gym?" She grins mischievously.

"He would have made it there in two minutes flat."

"Well, it's a good thing you aren't at risk of having a dad bod any time soon. I'd hate to lose you to the gym." Her hands travel over my chest. "Although, whatever you're doing is most certainly working for you."

"Glad you approve," I say as I start walking out of the water.

"Where are we going? You can put me down you know. I have legs."

"Back to the room. And I don't want to put you down." My hands squeeze the fleshy globes of her ass as I make my way back to the room. I really need to remember to cut this bikini up.

Chapter Fifteen

Ella

DEAN CARRIES me straight through our room and into the shower. He doesn't put me down until we're under the water. And even then, my feet are only on the floor long enough for him to undress me. He curses and mumbles something about buying new swimwear.

Right now, my back is currently shoved up against the cold tile wall. Dean is holding my body up like I weigh nothing, as he sucks and nibbles on my breasts. My back arches off the wall when he bites down on my right nipple, while twisting the other one between his fingers.

Fuck, I don't know what it is about being bitten. The pain of it is almost enough to send me over the edge alone, without anything else. I'm going to have to remember to talk to my therapist about this.

I'm not sure it's a healthy thing for me to be wanting.

All thoughts of therapists, and whether this is right or wrong, disappear out the window when Dean moves his mouth to my left breast. Without warning, his teeth are clamped down on my nipple.

"Fuck, that feels so good. Don't stop. No, stop. No, don't stop."

Dean chuckles around my nipple. My hands are pulling or pushing on his head. I can't decide if I want more or less of what he's doing right now. He takes his mouth away from my nipple, the little *plop* sound echoing in the shower.

His tongue licks up the side of my neck. "Mmm, you taste so fucking good, babe."

"Uh-huh." I'm out of my mind with need. All I can think of is being filled and stretched again. "Dean, I need you inside me now."

"Are you sure? You're not too sore from last night?" Dean asks, although he's already lining the head of his cock up with my opening. Tightening my legs around his waist, I bring myself down on him.

"I'm positive. I'm not a fucking wilting flower, Dean." A loud moan escapes me as he bottoms out inside of me. The slight twinge of pain quickly gives way to pleasure as my walls convulse around him.

"Fuck, Ella. Hold on tight, babe. Things are about to get rough," he warns as he pushes my back harder into the wall, my arms and legs clinging on to him as tightly as I can.

Dean starts to fuck me. Literally, it's like a crazed animal has been let loose. He thrusts in and out, quick and hard. My head falls back, hitting the tiles. My eyes roll back into my head. I wouldn't be surprised if the whole island can hear my screams right now.

Dean brings a hand up to my throat, holding my head still as he continues to plunge in and out. I'm so close to coming. "I'm going to… oh fuck!" I yell out as Dean's hand tightens around my throat. I open my eyes; he's staring intently at my face.

My mouth is hanging open and my chest is starting to burn. That's how I find my orgasm. Dean's hand loosens as my walls spasm around him. He grunts as warm spurts of him fill me.

My whole body shakes as I try to find the strength to continue holding onto him. Dean turns around and sits down on the floor of the shower. He doesn't let go of me. He doesn't pull out. I can feel his cock twitching inside of me.

We sit like that, catching our breath while basking in the afterglow of that orgasmic release. We hold onto each other. I want to stay like this forever.

"I wish I had known it felt this good," I say.

"Mmhmm, why is that?" Dean asks as he nuzzles his face in my neck.

"Because I would have tried harder to get you in my bed years ago."

"You would have got me killed is what you would have done. All those years of wanting you and not being able to touch you, it was fucking pure torture."

"Oh, trust me. I know the feeling."

SITTING on the patio drinking a mimosa, I'm mesmerised by the view as the waves roll in and out. I love the ocean. It's always been my dream to have a beach house. There's something about it that's just so peaceful, the smell of the salt in the air, and the relaxing sounds of crashing waves.

Which is the total opposite to watching Dean on the sand, pacing up and down the beach. He's been on the phone for over thirty minutes. I can't hear what he's talking about, but whatever it is, he looks stressed.

Deciding not to wait for him any longer, I dig out my laptop. I can use this time to get some work done. We're not meeting up with everyone else until lunch time. That will give me a few hours of work time. Well, at least until Dean finishes with his call, really.

I log into the remote servers for the club and pull up the spreadsheets I've been working on. I've narrowed down that the accounts for the bars are off. I've managed to track each date that money has been missing. The new cash registers that Zac had installed a couple of years back are connected to Wi-Fi. They upload data to the club's servers after each transaction, giving each night a total figure.

Zac never bothered to tell the staff about this feature. I'm not one hundred percent sure he even realises that the system does this. He still has the bar managers counting the tills and keeping digital ledgers each night. I'm halfway through matching the nights with missing funds to the staff rosters — who was covering those shifts and who was signing off on the nights' earnings.

I've accounted for over one hundred and fifty thousand dollars that's been stolen in the last twelve months. I have a really good hunch who it could be. I just don't want to believe it's this person. I want to prove myself wrong. That's why I'm still digging, looking for any evidence that it's not her. It just can't be her.

How could someone so close to our family betray us like that. If she needed help, she could have just asked. Most people wouldn't know this, but Zac would help out anyone that needs it. He's always trying to find ways to help others. He just usually does it anonymously. He doesn't want recognition for it.

The other day, I saw a transaction for a donation of one million dollars he made out to the breast cancer association. When I asked him about it, he told me if I wanted to keep my job, I wouldn't tell anyone. I know his threats of firing me are empty. There's no way he would. I mean, I'm almost certain they're empty threats. But I'm not about to push the boundaries to find out either.

Growing up, I was always the good child. I tried my hardest in school. I stayed away from trouble as much as I could. I never stayed out late. I did everything I could to make it easier for Zac. What twenty-year-old wants to be dumped with the job of raising his younger siblings?

Zac never complained though. He always made sure Bray and I had everything we could ever need or want. He was there at all of my school's parent-teacher meetings. Although, thinking back on it, my teachers were all overly friendly with Zac. I wouldn't be surprised if he hooked up with half of them.

As I'm going through the staff roster, checking off who was working on the dates in question, my computer freezes. A message screen pops up. What the hell is happening? Did I open a window somewhere? I'm clicking the escape button, trying to get out of the window, when the text appears.

It's like someone is typing in real time, each letter of each word appearing on the screen. The words are all in caps; the message they convey is loud and clear.

PEOPLE WHO LOOK FOR MISSING LINKS TEND TO FIND THEMSELVES MISSING!!!! STOP LOOKING!!!!!

My eyebrows draw down in confusion. Why

would someone be sending me this? The lightbulb goes off and I slam my laptop closed. I can feel the panic creeping up under my skin. My breathing increases; my heart beats faster and faster. I need to escape.

I look up and see Dean still on the phone. He's looking back at me. I smile and wave. I can't ruin this weekend for him. He put so much thought into giving me the perfect getaway. I refuse to allow my panic to ruin it.

I'm cold and shivering as I make my way back inside. Whoever's stealing from the club knows that I know. They want to shut me up. I can't go back to living where I'm scared of my own shadow, waiting for the bogeyman to jump out and grab me.

But that bogeyman just became all too real. Someone does want to jump out and grab me. I throw the laptop on the bed and head straight for the bathroom. I'm digging through the cabinets and searching for a razor before I even know what I'm doing.

It's not until I'm holding the blade between my fingers that some part of my subconscious kicks in and tells me to stop, that voice in the back of my head telling me I don't need to do this. I shove it aside though, not listening to a word of what it says.

I know it's the wrong choice. The moment the blade connects with skin, the moment the pain takes over, my mind drifts off into the hazy fog. I know I shouldn't have done it. But why the hell does something so damn wrong, feel so right?

Sitting on the bathroom floor, I drop the razor to the ground. Pulling some toilet paper off the roll, I hold it over my forearm. It's not a big cut. But as the haze wears off, the full reality of what I've just done sinks in. Fuck. I need Bray. I need to call Bray. He will know what to do. He'll be able to help.

I'm about to get up and go search for my phone when Dean bursts through the bathroom door. He takes one look at me on the floor. His eyes scan over my body, stopping on the blade that fell by my feet. He doesn't say anything.

He walks in, picks me up and takes me to the bed. Dean sits with his back against the headboard and holds me, straddled over his lap. His hands run up and down my back, and through my hair. His gentle, comforting caresses break me. The silent tears stream freely down my face.

We sit like this in silence. As I fall apart, yet again, in this man's arms. How many nights did he hold me like this until I fell asleep when I was eighteen? Countless.

He deserves so much better than a broken Princess for a girlfriend. "I'm so sorry," I whisper.

"Ella, you have nothing to be sorry about, babe."

"You're wrong. I'm sorry that I'm so broken. I'm sorry that after six months I caved in at the first sign of trouble. I'm sorry I can't be the girlfriend you deserve. I'm sorry that I broke my promise to come and find you when I felt the urge to cut, just hours after making that promise. I'm sorry."

"Look at me," Dean commands as he places his finger under my chin and straightens my head so that I'm facing him.

"You have nothing to be sorry about. No, you're not the girlfriend I deserve. You are so much more than I will ever be deserving of. You are not broken; there is not a damn thing about you that I would change. You didn't break a promise, Princess. You promised you would try to reach out to me for help, not that you always would. You are my everything, Ella. Always have. Always will. These hurdles that life is throwing us, they will only make us stronger. They will not break us. Nothing can break us. We will get through this together. I promise."

"I love you. I don't know how to put it into words, but you are my everything too. Always have. Always will," I say as I lean up and kiss him.

After sitting on the bed for a while, I climb off and search for my phone. Dean watches me the whole time. Once I find it, I look back at him. I should be able to talk to him about this. I know that I can tell him anything. In theory, I know that anyway. But right now, the one person I want to talk to is my brother.

"Call him, Ella. It's okay," Dean says, already knowing who I want to call. A wave of relief washes over me. I didn't realise I was trying to find a way to tell him I wanted to call Bray.

"Thank you," I whisper.

"Babe, he's your brother. If you need him, call him. Don't ever think that you can't go talk to him whenever you need to." Dean walks over and kisses me on the forehead. "I'll be on the patio if you need me."

I nod, unable to form words right now.

Sitting on the floor, with my back against the bed, I dial Bray. The phone rings and rings. I'm about to hang up, thinking it's going to ring out, when he answers, breathless.

"Ella, what's up?"

Why am I calling him? He's on holiday too. Why am I ruining everyone's weekend? I bring my knees up to my chest.

"Ella?" Bray asks.

When I still don't answer, he asks me the one question I never fail to respond to. "Ella, sweetheart, how long?" His voice is quiet. I can hear the uncertainty in his words.

"A few hours," I whisper.

"Where are you? I'm on my way."

"No, you don't need to come here. I just… I don't know."

"Don't move. I'll be there in a minute," he says.

"Okay." I hang up the phone. I don't hear Dean come back inside and sit down next to me. I feel his arms wrap around me. I hear his promises whispered in my ear.

Chapter Sixteen

Dean

THE IMAGE of Ella sitting on the bathroom floor... A razor dropped at her feet... Holding tissue paper over her forearm... This image is fucking haunting me. I don't know what I'm doing here. I don't know how to fucking help her.

I wish I could be the one she leans on. The first one she thinks of to call when she needs help with this. It's killing me that I'm not. But I can't let her know that. I'm not that much of a fucking asshole. I know that Bray's been the one to be there through the years. I've got no one to blame for that but myself.

I made the choice that put all of these events into motion. If I hadn't left her, maybe she wouldn't have turned to such drastic measures to escape the pain. To escape the memories that torture her. I hold her in my arms, not knowing what the fuck to say to make it better.

Bray barges through the front door of the villa. He spots us sitting on the floor. He stands there, watching. I know he's pissed. I also know he's blaming me for not stopping her in time. He wouldn't be wrong. It is my fault. I shouldn't have left her side. I knew something was wrong the moment she smiled and waved at me.

"Ella, Princess. Bray's here." I kiss her forehead. She picks her head up and looks at Bray. She doesn't move. I know I've got to let her go. That I need to remove myself from the room so she can talk to Bray. I don't want to. But I will for her.

"I'm going to be on the patio. Will you be okay?" I ask her. She nods her head.

Standing with Ella still in my arms, I sit her on the bed before I walk out to the patio. I shut the door, giving them the privacy they need.

Around thirty minutes later, Bray comes out and sits on the chair opposite me. He's silent for a moment as he looks me over. Letting out a sigh, he tells me, "It's not your fault, you know."

I shrug. "It is. I shouldn't have left her alone. I was down on the beach on a call. I kept looking back up, watching her. I should have come back up sooner when she went inside."

"It's not your fault. As much as I'd love to place the blame on someone, we can't. It's not fair to Ella to walk around blaming people for what's going on inside her own head. She's come so far in the two years she's been getting help. This… this is just a little bump in the road. She will overcome this."

"I know." I shake my head. "What am I meant to do, man? How do I help her with this?"

"You be there to pick her up when she falls. You learn to recognise the signs that she's not coping well. These attacks of hers usually come on fast and can pass just as quickly."

"I know. I've seen her panic attacks. But this… She walked inside looking fine. Smiling. Two minutes later, I find her on the bathroom floor, a razor dropped at her feet. What the fuck happened to make her lose control?"

Bray shakes his head. "It's not about her losing control. She does this to take the control back. She only cuts when she's feeling out of control. I don't know what happened. She wouldn't tell me, which is fucking strange. She always tells me."

I look behind me. Ella is in the kitchenette making coffee. She seems okay.

"What was she doing before she walked inside?" Bray asks.

"She was sitting here on her laptop." Her laptop that's on the floor at the end of the bed. Fuck. Why didn't I think of that earlier?

"Well, whatever it was that set her off, it's more than likely on that laptop. Think you can go distract her while I grab it?" Bray asks.

I'm already picking up my tablet, which I left on the table earlier. "There's no need. I can see everything that happens on the club servers. Whatever she was doing, she would have been on the servers."

Pulling up the feeds from the previous hour, right around the time Ella was sitting out here, I dig through the files until I find the ones with her login on them. "Looks like she was looking at staffing rosters from the past twelve months." I don't mention the name that seems to pop up the most in the data she's collated on her spreadsheet. If she's uncovered that this person is the one stealing from the club, I'm not sure how that fucking betrayal will go down.

What else were you looking at, Ella? Another folder further down has her name next to it. The folder's untitled. Clicking it open, I read the message that pops up on the screen of my tablet.

"What the fuck!" I yell, causing Bray to jump up to look at what I'm reading.

PEOPLE WHO LOOK FOR MISSING LINKS TEND TO FIND THEMSELVES MISSING!!!! STOP LOOKING!!!!!

"What is that?" he asks, puzzled.

"Someone is not happy Ella is digging around in the club's accounts."

"Some fucker sent that shit to Ella?" Now he's yelling.

Why wouldn't she tell me about this? I don't get it. She shouldn't be keeping this sort of shit to herself.

I click around in the file for a bit, satisfied that this was sent from Sydney. From inside the club, to be precise. The sender, that fucker is going to wish they never met the Williamson's.

Storming inside, I'm about to ask Ella about the message when she looks over her shoulder and smiles. A genuine happy smile.

"Want a coffee? I just made some."

"Ah, no. I'm good, babe." I look to Bray and he shakes his head. We're in agreement that we won't bring this up right now.

"Okay, nugget. I'll see you at lunch," Bray says to Ella, ruffling her hair as he walks by her.

He stops at the door and asks, "Do either of you know why Zac's been holed up in the gym all morning? Grunting something about a dad bod?"

Ella bursts out laughing before batting her lashes and replying, "No, I wouldn't have a clue."

"You're the worst fucking liar I've ever met, El."
With that, Bray walks out the door, leaving Ella and me alone. We have exactly forty minutes before we have to meet the others at lunch. I know what I want to do.

"Princess, put some shoes on. I wanna show you something."

"Almost there. It's just up over this hill." I pull on Ella's hand behind me, as she curses and swats flies and mosquitoes away from her.

"Dean, when you said you wanted to show me something, I was kind of hoping it was your cock. Not a bug-infested forest a thousand miles away."

"Princess, we've been walking for two minutes. Literally, two minutes. And look. We're here."

Down the slight hill is a little water hole. Crystal clear calm water. It's surrounded by rainforest. A little hidden bit of paradise. I may hate the beach, but I fucking love being in nature like this. Surrounded by trees, by wildlife, this is peace.

"Want to go for a quick dip before lunch?" I ask. Ella's already throwing her shirt on the ground and undoing her shorts before I even finish the question. Guess that means we're getting in then.

"Last one in's a rotten egg!" Ella shrieks as she runs barefoot towards the edge of the water. She stops just before she touches the water.

"Wait. Dean, how do we know if there's crocs in here or not?" She bites her bottom lip. I laugh. She's worried about getting in this clear water, but has no drama diving headfirst into the ocean? That makes a lot of sense.

"You can't be serious?" I laugh, which does not go over too well with her. I get her famous death glare in return.

"Are you really laughing at me right now?" she grits out between clenched teeth.

One thing about Ella, she's never been a fan of being laughed at. Ever. When she was fourteen, she filled Bray's hair gel tube with super glue. All because he laughed at her when she cried about getting a B on her English test. Bray ended up having to shave his head.

"No! I am not laughing at you, Princess. I would never." As much as I try not to laugh, I can't help it. Her pout, her clenched fists, she's just so fucking adorable.

I take her face in both my hands, and my lips meet hers. "You're so fucking sexy when you're mad. Come on." Entwining our fingers together, I pull her into the water. "Besides, I'm not about to share my meal with any crocs."

Ella's body relaxes as she floats around on top of the water. I really need to start carrying a camera with me. She's so fucking beautiful. Her full breasts barely contained by a black bikini top. Her tanned skin, glistening in the sun. My eyes travel down her body. Her flat stomach. Her long, toned legs. My cock is painfully fucking hard. *Again.*

Grasping one of her ankles, I pull her towards me. She straightens up. Her legs instinctually wrap around my waist. I want nothing more than to sink my cock inside her again. But we have a lunch to get to. And I have some answers she needs to give me.

Picking up her arm, I kiss over the small cut that she's placed a band-aid over. "I need you to tell me what happened? Why did you feel like you had to do this?" I ask. I already know why, but I need to hear it from her. I need her to trust me enough to tell me everything.

"I..." I watch as her mouth opens and closes. She's not sure if she should tell me.

"Babe, you know anything you tell me will stay between us. It's just you and me. We're in this together now. You don't need to do things alone."

"I know. It's just... I'm so close to finding out who's been stealing from the club. Actually, that's not right. I know who's been doing it. I just want to find evidence to convince me I'm wrong."

"Okay, who do you think it is?"

"What if I'm wrong, Dean? If I come out and

accuse this person, it would devastate Alyssa. I can't do that if I could be wrong."

"Do you think you're wrong?"

Ella shakes her head no. "But I could be."

"Ella, you are the smartest person I know. You're not wrong about this." I try to reassure her. As much as I want her to be wrong, I don't think she is.

"But the message… I just don't believe that this person would send such a message to me. Stealing is one thing. Threatening to kill someone is totally different."

"People who feel cornered are dangerous, babe. You'd be surprised what they can be capable of."

She tilts her head at me. "You already know, don't you?"

See, the smartest person I know. Nothing gets past her, ever. I nod my head.

"And you've seen the message I received this morning?"

"I have." My jaw clenches. "I promise that I will not let anything happen to you, Ella. I just got you. I'm not going to lose you to some psycho, greedy fucking thief."

"How am I meant to go to work? They know I know. Maybe I should just tell Zac. Have them arrested," she suggests.

"Do you trust me?"

"More than anyone." She doesn't miss a beat with her response, even if I know it's inflated. The people she trusts the most in the world are her brothers. And that's how it should be. I'm glad she's got those two assholes in her life.

"Let's not tell anyone yet. Let's enjoy the weekend. You're safe here. That message was sent from inside the club. Which means, whoever sent it, they're still in Sydney."

"Okay, let's enjoy the weekend. I really like my present by the way."

"What present?" I ask. I haven't given her anything yet.

"The island getaway weekend. You didn't have to do all this. I would have been happy with a mug or chocolate."

I laugh. There is no way I would have gotten away with giving her a mug. "Yeah, okay, I'll remember to get you a mug for your birthday next year. I'm sure that will go over well. But this isn't your gift. Your gift is back home. You'll have to wait to get it."

"Well, I love it already."

"You don't even know what it is." I laugh. I don't think I've ever laughed so much before. "Come on, we need to get to lunch. Next time, remind me to leave everyone else at home. I don't like sharing you."

"That's the best idea you've ever had."

Chapter Seventeen

Ella

WE GET to the restaurant for lunch. Bray and Reilly are already there waiting. They are seated on opposite sides of the table with the twins sitting in highchairs at the end of the table next to them. Reilly looks drop-dead gorgeous; she's wearing a black sheer coverall with a bright yellow bikini underneath.

To look at her, you would not think she had twins. She's a little curvier than she used to be, but those curves stuck to the right places. I'm envious of her pale complexion. She looks even more pale when she's near Bray, who's more tanned and olive-toned.

Thankfully, the twins get their looks from their mother, just with darker features. They've got big beautiful green eyes, each with a thick head of dark red curls.

"Hey," I say before taking a seat next to Bray,

while Dean takes the seat next to Reilly. I'd much rather be sitting next to Dean, but that would have been odd, to leave Bray sitting on one side of the table by himself.

I can't meet Bray's eyes right now. Does he think I've failed again? That we're starting back at day one? Technically, we are. But I feel okay right now. I don't need to keep cutting. I'm going to keep saying that in my head until I believe it.

One thing I noticed today, when I did cut, it felt good. But it didn't feel as good as it used to. I couldn't help but compare it to when Dean hurts me—well, when he dishes out slight pain to get me off. We haven't discussed that yet. But I know that conversation's coming.

Is that going to be my new addiction? Sex with a side of pain? I'm not opposed to lots of sex with Dean, but what if it's not healthy? The way I like sex, I'm sure it's not normal. Maybe I should ask Bray? If anyone's competent to give sex advice, it'd be him. He had a revolving door of women before Reilly.

Bray reaches under the table and takes hold of my hand. I didn't notice I was wringing my hands together on my lap. He gives a little squeeze, but doesn't let go. I look up to see everyone looking at me. Did I say something out loud?

"Where's Zac and Alyssa?" I ask just as they walk through the door. Alyssa looks grumpy, and Zac looks… tired.

"So sorry we're late. How are you?" Alyssa comes

to my side of the table, hugging me before sitting next to me.

Her eyes drop to my lap, and to Bray's hand still holding mine. She smiles gently at me but doesn't say anything. I wonder if they all know. Did Bray tell them I relapsed? I look over to him and he gives me a slight head shake no.

I'm starting to think all these assholes are telepathic. How do they keep doing that? Knowing what I'm thinking, without me having to say anything?

"What took you guys so long? Bad traffic?" Bray directs at Zac.

"Something like that," Zac says as he sits down next to Alyssa.

Okay, so apparently, I'm the only one that cares about having even numbers of people on each side of the table. Ash sits next to Dean, playing on an iPad. He's using his finger to draw pictures — well, scribbling, really — on the screen.

"Oh, come on. No, your idiot brother here has been in the gym all morning. Ash and I had to literally drag him out of there fifteen minutes ago."

"You've been in the gym all morning? Why would you do that, Zac? Haven't you heard? We're on a weekend holiday. Now's the time to indulge, not workout," I say sweetly.

"Shut it," Zac replies, pointing a fork at me.

Dean coughs, in an attempt to hold in a laugh. "Really, man, why you gotta be that fucking vain? Just grow old gracefully."

"We're the same fucking age, idiot," Zac grumbles back at Dean. Alyssa slaps him on the chest.

"Language," she scolds at both Zac and Dean.

"Daddy said bad word." Ash sticks his head up to dob in Zac momentarily.

"We really need to have a chat about the bro code, little man," Bray tells Ash.

"You know, Zac, we may be the same age and all. But I happen to have it on good authority that I do not have anything close to resembling a dad bod." Dean sends a wink in my direction.

"Nope, not even close. The things I wanna do with that body…" My thoughts trail off. Bray lets go of my hand, like I've burned him.

"Gross, Ella, never — and I mean fucking *never* — say anything like that around me again."

"But you always tell me I can talk to you about anything, Bray?" I remind him, my voice dripping with sugary innocence.

Bray sighs while rubbing a hand down his face. "Yeah, I know."

"Hang on!" Alyssa shouts, causing us all to look in her direction.

"You spent all bloody morning in the gym because you think you have a dad bod? You idiot!" She laughs at him.

"No, I did not. I just felt like working out." Zac tries to lie. When Alyssa raises her eyebrows at him, giving him that don't fuck with me look, he caves — just like he always does with her.

"Okay, but it's Ella's fault. She's the one that told me I have a dad bod," Zac pouts.

"Oh my god! You are an idiot. Have you looked in the mirror? There's not an ounce of fat on you. Those grooves on your abdomen, that's called a six-pack, hunny. You do not have a dad bod. Ella, tell him he doesn't have a dad bod."

Alyssa looks at me pleadingly. She wants me to put him out of his misery. Yeah, that's not going to happen.

"Lyssa, I know you're Zac's number one fan. So, chances are you're blind to the truth. But he very much has a dad bod." I shrug. In my mind, I'm not even lying. He is a dad, and he has a body: dad bod.

"No, don't listen to her, hunny. You are still GQ worthy. I'm the one that knows your body better than anyone. If you had a dad bod, I'd tell you," Alyssa says. Zac shrugs his shoulders, pouting.

He's such a bloody baby. I should put him out of his misery. But where would the fun be in that?

"Okay, this is stupid. Zac, you don't have a fucking dad bod. I mean, you even give Bray a run for his money and that man is fine with a capital F." Reilly laughs. "Honestly, do you know how many staff I had to warn off when I was working at the club? Pretty much all of them; they were very pathetic, really. I mean, you're cute and all, but that whole brooding attitude is a bore."

I thought she was finished with her spiel. Picking

up the glass of champagne that's in front of me, I take a sip. Reilly chooses this time to speak again.

"Besides, Ella's cock blind at the moment. The only body she cares about seeing is grouch number two over here. Give it time, it'll wear off. Maybe." Reilly shrugs her shoulders.

My champagne comes spitting out of my mouth. Did she really just say I was cock blind?

"Cock blind? What does that even mean, Reilly?" I ask

Bray and Zac both groan, very loudly.

"Babe, stop. Don't mention my little sister and cock in the same sentence."

"Okay, Ash, come with mummy, sweetie. We're going to go have a look at that fish tank. And when we come back, all inappropriate language better be finished with." Alyssa uses her expertly honed in mum voice on all of us.

"Okay, cock blind, little El, means you've become so taken by this lover boy over here that you don't see or notice anyone else. You're hungry for what the big guy gives you." Reilly looks Dean up and down, then back at me.

"I mean, I don't blame you. He's a little rough around the edges and could use a shave. But I've seen what's hiding under that shirt and I approve." She winks.

This is one time I'm thankful for my olive complexion. I would otherwise be beet red from embarrassment right now. I would normally feel jealousy when another woman checks out Dean. But when Reilly just did, I didn't feel like that at all. I actually think she's saying that to rile up Bray.

It's clearly worked. He's currently twitching his leg up and down under the table. His fists are clenched. And he's directing his icy cold stare towards Dean.

"Unca Bray. Unca Bray. Look!" Ash yells out from the other side of the restaurant. Bray gets up and walks over to the fish tank to see what he's being summoned for.

The rest of lunch went down very PG. I think we are a little too afraid of Alyssa to go against her no swear order. Dean has us all booked in for a reef tour on a glass bottom boat in forty minutes. I'm so excited to see the reef. I've always wanted to come out here.

Everyone's leaving the restaurant at the same time. I need to steal Bray away so I can ask him about some stuff. I know I can talk to Dean about it, but honestly, I'm so worried that he's going to leave me again. I've tried so hard to be the girlfriend he deserves. And I failed, royally, at that today.

I'm also afraid of hearing the truth. What if he

thinks my need for pain during sex is odd? I wish I had girlfriends to talk about this sort of stuff with. I could probably talk to Reilly or Alyssa. I know they would listen and offer advice. But it's awkward.

The only person I've ever been able to talk to, without embarrassment about anything, is Bray. He's always been the one I have heart to hearts with. Don't get me wrong, if I wanted to, Zac would absolutely take the time to talk with me. He would hate every single minute of it, but he would try.

When I was fourteen, I got my first period. Yes, I was a late bloomer. Zac tried to give me the whole birds and bees chat. He tried to explain about how my body was changing, about what I had to do. He tried. And he failed big time. He got so flustered when he tried to tell me I was becoming a woman. He demanded that I just stop growing up, that I stay his little Ella. He didn't want me to become a woman.

That's when Bray walked in on the conversation, took me by the hand and led me into his room. We sat on his bed for hours that night. He told me everything he knew about the female body. He told me that just because I could have sex, didn't mean I should. Clearly, I held on to that piece of advice.

When I was sixteen, Bray took me to the GP and got me on the contraceptive pill. I tried to tell him I wasn't interested in having sex. It was a lie. I totally wanted to bone the hell out of Dean by then. It was never going to happen though.

Bray convinced me that it was better to be safe

than sorry. He then took me to a group centre for teen mums. After that day, I have not missed a day of taking that little pill.

I just need to find an excuse to get him away from everyone else. Then it hits me.

"Oh, crap. Bray, you were meant to show me that thing in the gym you told me about." I implore him with my eyes.

Bray laughs before agreeing with me. "Shit, yeah. Sorry, Sis, I forgot all about it. Want to go in there now?"

I nod my head.

"Dean, Bro, you wouldn't mind helping Reilly back to the villa with the girls, would you? Thanks, man. We'll meet you all at the jetty in forty," Bray says as he starts pulling me away by the hand.

We bypass the gym. Bray leads me around the resort until he finds a spot he deems suitable. The garden we stopped in has a gazebo. We head for that and both sit down with our backs against the railings.

"Okay, spill it. What's so important you had to drag me away? You know, I had a seventy percent chance of getting laid while the girls were taking a nap just now."

"Well, shit. Sorry. And I actually mean that." I never used to care about being a cock block to Bray. "I mean, now that I know how good sex actually is, I am sorry for all those times I cock blocked you. Kind of."

"Wait. Shut the front door? Rewind the fuck up. You had sex?" he yells.

"Thanks, Bray. I don't think they heard you in Perth. Do you want to shout it out a bit louder?" Sarcasm drips from my lips. Maybe I should have just kept this to myself. I should just talk to my therapist about it. I look down at my shirt, my hands wringing in the hem.

Bray sighs, then shuffles around to sit cross-legged in front of me. He takes my hands in his and stops them from fidgeting.

"I'm sorry. You just took me by surprise, that's all. You're so young, El. You don't need to be having sex yet," he says so seriously.

"Bray, I'm twenty-three. Losing your V-card at twenty-three is not young by any means."

He shrugs his shoulders and smirks at me. "It was worth a shot. So, who was it? Do I know him?" He has the best bloody poker face, because as he asks this question, he legitimately looks serious, like he doesn't know who it was.

"Seriously, don't be an idiot. You know it was Dean." As much as I tell him not to be an idiot, his jokes do settle my nerves — a lot.

"Okay, did you like it? Do I need to kick his ass? Is he treating you right?" He fires question after question at me.

"Oh, I like it. I like it a lot. You're not allowed to kick his ass, or any part of his body for that matter.

And it's Dean. Are you really questioning if he treats me right?"

"I have to ask. Because, frankly, I'd love for you to give me a reason to punch the fucker again."

When I don't respond, he clarifies that he's only joking. I don't know how to broach the subject of what I really need to know.

"Okay, so you had sex. With Dean. What's going on in that pretty little head, El? What's wrong?"

"Do you think I'm too broken to be a good girl-friend? I've never been someone's girlfriend before. What if the things I like are too weird for him?"

"First, you're not broken. Dean is counting his lucky stars that he has you. Trust me — I've seen him counting the stars. What things are we talking about here, El?"

"I like pain, Bray. That can't be normal," I admit.

"That's not a secret. And if Dean can't handle you the way you are, then that's his loss. You had one slip in six months, Ella. That's not weird. We knew that there is no telling when everything's going to get to be too much. We can't predict when you're going to slip up. That doesn't make you weird."

"No, it's not that. During sex, Bray, I like pain. It's almost like I need it to, you know…"

"Oh, well, that's normal. Everyone has kinks. As much as I really don't want to fucking know this… What are we talking about? A light spanking? Whips and chains? Floggers?"

"Ah, no. I don't know. I just know, when he bites

into my skin, it's like a thousand bolts of pleasure go through me. The first time he, you know… It hurt, but it hurt so good. That can't be normal, can it?"

"Trust me, it's more than normal. You're getting in your own head, El. I've been with a lot of chicks; most of them liked being bitten somewhere during sex."

"Okay. Thank you."

"Why aren't you talking to Dean about this?" he asks.

My shoulders move up and down. "What if he thinks I'm weird? What if he can't handle my broken pieces and he leaves me again? I don't think I'll get through that again."

"Babe, unfortunately, that boy is not going anywhere. He couldn't be more in love with you if he tried. You're stuck with him now. I really hope you do love his ugly ass, because we might have to bury him to get rid of him if you don't."

"I do. I've never stopped loving him. I'm just so afraid he's going to leave again."

"You need to tell him how you're feeling, El. It's not fair to him to keep him shut out. You know I'll always have time for you. You know that no matter what, you can talk to me about anything. But you also have Dean now. He should be the one you turn to first for everything. He should be your partner in everything."

"Okay, I'll talk to him."

"He loves you, Ella. As much as he knows you

need to talk to me, it's clear it's hurting him that you're not talking to him."

"I don't mean to. It's just easy with you. You don't judge me, and I'm not afraid you're going to leave me. No matter how much I might wish you would sometimes."

"Never ever. God, imagine if Zac was your only sibling. You'd be a lost cause, that's for sure."

We both laugh as we stand up and make our way to the jetty.

Chapter Eighteen

Dean

I WATCH as Ella and Bray make their way to the jetty. I'm suddenly nervous and I don't fucking know why. I know she talks to Bray about everything. She always has. But I want to be the one she turns to when she needs someone to talk to.

Why would she not talk to me about things? I don't know what else I can do to reassure her that I'm here for her. Always. I know we will get there soon. I just have to work harder on building her trust back. She might say she trusts me, but she's holding back.

It's almost like she's waiting for something to go wrong with us. Well, fuck that. I won't fucking let it. I've just got to work harder. I need to be patient with her. It's my own damn fault. If I hadn't made that choice to let her go four years ago, she wouldn't be doubting my commitment now.

I wonder how she'd feel about a more permanent commitment. If I whisked her off and made her Mrs. McKinley, would she want that? Would that be enough to prove to her that I'm not going anywhere?

Her smile is bright as she reaches me. Her arm wraps around my waist. I cling to her, probably a little tighter than I should. She doesn't complain. No, she lets out a little sigh, leaning her head on my chest. My chin comes to rest on top of her head.

Bray gives me an odd look as he walks past us and towards Reilly and the twins, who are strapped into a stroller contraption thing. I can't read his expression, but it's a mix between being pissed and not wanting to be pissed. I don't have time, nor do I care to figure him out right now. I have Ella in my arms; everything in my world is right again.

"You ready to go see the reef, Princess?" I ask.

Her head nods against my chest. "So ready." She tilts her head back and smiles up at me. "I love you so damn much."

I lean in and kiss her, gently, slowly. Breaking the kiss off way quicker than I would have liked, I tell her, "I love you too. Always have. Always will."

Letting my arms drop from around her, I take hold of her hand, entwining our fingers together. "Come on, let's go see this reef I've heard so much about."

Ella's excitement is contagious as she jumps up and down on the boat.

"I swear you're going to break the glass bottom.

Sit your ass down, El. These princesses, as advanced as they are, can't swim yet. It's their one flaw." Bray sighs. He likes to think his kids are genuine geniuses. I don't see it. All I see is drool and spit up.

"Bray, no baby their age can bloody swim," Ella says in defence of her nieces.

"Ash could." Zac smirks, sticking his chest out like the proud father he is.

"That's because Ash is a fu… genius child," I say, quickly muffling my "inappropriate" language before Alyssa can scold me. Because if any child is a genius, it's that one. He's smart as shit for someone so young.

"Please, you just wait. My girls are going to be the smartest people around. They're probably going to cure world hunger or some shit. The next Mother Teresa in the making!" Bray declares.

He's been claiming that they're going to be nuns since Reilly was pregnant with them. I can't wait for the day they start bringing boys home. That day, I'll make sure to have a fucking camera.

The boat comes to a stop. We're literally in the middle of the ocean; the only land in sight is a small sand dune island not too far from where we've stopped. There are two young guys that are staffing the boat. One of them opens a metal storage trunk sitting along one side.

"There's snorkelling gear in here. It's a great spot. You'll be able to see reef sharks, sea turtles—the coral life is amazing here. You'll also find yourself a few

Nemos and Dorys if you go down close up to the coral."

Ella squeals as she rips her shirt over her head before yanking her shorts down. The guy who's trying to give directions stops talking, mouth open wide, while he openly gawks at my girl.

"Mate, you have exactly three seconds to avert your eyes from her before I make sure you end up as shark bait," I snarl.

The guy looks at me with shock, then a challenging smirk comes across his face. He thinks he can take me. The fucker has no idea what I'm capable of. I've killed for much less of a crime than someone ogling my girl. I'd take pleasure in choking that smile off his face right now.

"I wouldn't, mate. I've seen him in action. It's not pretty. Besides, that is my little sister. If he doesn't slit your throat, you can be certain I will."

Alyssa just put headphones on Ash; she's taken to carrying around a set of headphones with his iPad lately. Probably wise. The kid's going to have a vocabulary worse than a sailor by the time he's five.

"Sit down and shut up. Both of you. You're being ridiculous." Ella points at me and Bray. She then turns to the guy with a sweet smile.

"I want to go snorkelling. I can't wait. Thank you." She picks up a set of flippers, goggles and a snorkel.

"Ah, yeah. Okay. Sam over here can take you over to the sand dune. There's loads of buckets and toys for the kids already there. You can't see it from here, but around the other side of the dune, there is a hut with shade."

"Great, Reilly and I will head over there with the kids. You three morons behave. Have fun snorkelling, Ella," Alyssa directs us all.

While Alyssa and Reilly are settling into a little boat that's attached at the side of this larger one, Zac looks torn. He wants to stay with Ella but also wants to go with Alyssa and Ash.

"Hey, El, I'm gonna give snorkelling a miss. I promised Ash some sandcastle time," he says before kissing her on her forehead.

"Sure. No worries. Take Bray with you. He's just going to dampen my fun anyway," Ella replies.

Zac laughs. "Okay. We'll see you guys over on the sand. If a shark comes, make sure you offer Dean up as a sacrifice and save yourself."

"Oh, I will. Don't worry." Ella winks at me.

Ella and I spent most of the afternoon in the water. She loved every minute of it. Her laughter and smiles greeted me the whole time, soothing my soul. I must admit we saw some amazing shit while snorkeling around the reef. I have to remember to bring her back here often.

She really needed this. By the time we make it to the little sand island, the afternoon sun is setting. I have plans for Ella tonight. Those plans do not include the rest of the crew.

We all head back to the boat. The ride back to the resort is quiet. The kids are all asleep by the time we make it to the jetty, each of us parting ways with plans to catch up tomorrow for breakfast before we start our trek back to Sydney.

I've ordered room service for dinner; I'm sitting on the patio waiting for Ella to finish in the shower. It's fucking hard for me not to stay in the bathroom with her. My skin is itching, my heart racing. What if she's not okay in there? I made sure to clear every single sharp object out of there. She can look all she wants; she won't find anything that she could use to cut with. It does not ease my rapid heartbeat as I wait for her to come out.

I'm ready to just head in there. How hard could it be to think of an excuse to go in there? Then again, Ella naked and soapy in the shower is enough of an excuse. My mind's made up. I stand up and am halfway across the room when the bathroom door opens.

Steam billows out of the door, surrounding the goddess who stands in the doorway. She's wearing one of my white shirts. It ends halfway down her thighs.

Her olive skin glistening, I can see her nipples harden under the fabric of the shirt. She's so fucking sexy.

"Fuck, Princess!" I run a hand down my face. I really want to pick her up, throw her on the bed and ravish her body. But it's more important that we have this dinner. I want to have a chat with her. I made a call to my lawyer while she was in the shower. I'll have the papers drawn up and ready to be signed by the time we get back to Sydney tomorrow.

I just need to get her to agree to sign them. I don't expect it to be an easy battle. Part of me hates myself for even suggesting that we do it this way. But there really is no time to go down the traditional route. I'll do anything to protect her; there is nothing I won't stop at.

Right now, making her a McKinley is one thing I can do. Nobody's stupid enough to fuck with the McKinley family. If they are, they usually find themselves out of breath. Literally.

My family may not be the mafia or mob, like Ella once asked about, but somehow, they're worse. They hide behind their dirty money. Growing up, the one thing I learnt from my father was that there is nothing money can't buy. And there are no limits to what people are capable of doing to keep hold of their wealth and luxurious lifestyles.

"What's wrong?" Ella's concerned voice drags me out of my own head.

"Apart from the fact that I have a raging hard-on

and I want to tie you to that bed and have my filthy way with you? Nothing's wrong," I deadpan.

"Well, that doesn't seem like a problem."

The white shirt sticks to her body. Her nipples are still hard and clearly visible through the damp fabric. No. We are having this dinner and this conversation. Reaching out, I grab hold of her wrist and pull her out to the patio. I purposefully sit on the other side of the small table. I want to be able to see her eyes, her face, when we have this conversation.

She's never been able to hide anything. Even when she tries to lie, or omit the truth even a little, her face twitches. Her eyes tend to roam the whole room. She has other tells too. Too many tells. Let's just say she gave up on learning to play poker only a month into trying to play. She was shit at it. But damn, did she look hot trying; even her fucking frustration at always losing was hot.

"Okay, so that's a no to the whole being tied to the bed thing?" Ella asks.

I swear she is testing my resolve, her eyes begging me to take her back inside and do whatever I want to her body.

"Not a no. Before the night is over, I promise, you will be tied to that bed, Princess." I smirk, as I watch her squirm in her seat.

"Eat. There are some things we need to discuss," I say, pointing to her food with my fork.

Her whole demeanor changes. Almost instantly, her body freezes up. But as quickly as she froze, she shakes it off. With a shaky voice, she asks, "What is it that you want to talk about?"

"Babe, relax. What's wrong?" I grab hold of her hand over the table.

"Well, I may be new at this. But even I know nothing good ever comes from the line *we need to talk*." She looks down, stabbing her food with her fork.

"What are your thoughts on marriage?" I blurt out, needing to test the waters. We've never had this conversation, aside from the comments I have dropped, and she's ignored. I'm hoping we are on the same wavelength here.

"That depends?" She shrugs.

"On what?"

"On who's getting married?"

"What if it was us?" I suggest, pointing between the two of us.

"Dean, are you proposing right now?"

"Babe, I'm not a fucking idiot. When I propose to you, I'll be sure to have a ring fitting of a fucking Queen."

"Okay, well, as long as there's a ring involved, I guess I'd be open to the idea." She laughs.

"You'd be open to the idea, huh?"

"Well, if someone else doesn't come at me with a ring before you get around to it, you're in with a fighting chance." Her smile lights up her face.

"If someone else tried to give you a ring, Ella…" I pause and wait for her to look up at me again. When she does, I deliver a promise I fully intend to carry through with. "I'd cut his fucking hands off, before ripping out his tongue."

She stares blankly at me for a long time, like she's trying to figure something out. "Why do I get the feeling you're not kidding?"

"Because I'm not." I shrug.

"Dean, you realise how crazy you sound, right?" she asks.

"Crazy about you, yeah." I smile, trying to ease some of her shock from my overly graphic proclamations. "Ella, you're not blind. And you sure as fuck are not stupid. You know I've done things that cross over the line of good and bad. I know there's a place in Hell waiting for me. I'm okay with that. But are you going to be?" I hold my breath waiting for her response.

"There isn't a damn thing I would change about you, Dean. I love you just as you are. And you're wrong. You are not going to Hell. We'll just stay right here, in purgatory together. Because, even in death, I will not let you leave me again."

"There is nothing that could possibly make me leave you, El."

Deciding to change the subject, I ask her what's been on my mind all day.

"What was it you had to talk to Bray about earlier today?"

Her cheeks heat up. Although her olive tone does a great job at hiding her blush, I can always tell when she's blushing. Her eyes divert, bouncing around the room. Her face begins to twitch.

"Don't even try to lie to me right now, Princess. I know you want to."

She lets out a huff. "Okay, you really want to know? Sex! I talked to Bray about sex, okay. Are you happy now?" she yells.

I drop my fork. It lands with a clank on my plate. "You spoke to your brother about sex?" I ask in disbelief.

Ella nods her head. "I don't exactly have a surplus of girlfriends lining up who I can talk to about these things. So, I talk to Bray."

"You spoke to your brother about sex? About the sex you have with me?" I ask again.

"Well, I'm not having sex with anyone else. So, yes." She sounds kind of annoyed with me at this point.

"You spoke to Bray about sex with me and I'm still alive? Shit, babe, it's lucky I wasn't fed to the sharks out there today." I point to the ocean in front of us.

Ella laughs. "Are you afraid of my brothers, Dean?"

"Not usually. But when it comes to you, those two assholes are unhinged." I shiver at the thought of the torture Bray is currently putting me through, even if it is only in his head.

"As opposed to you? You just threatened to cut off an imaginary man's hands and tongue." She points at me before scooping more rice onto her fork and shoving it in her mouth.

"I did." I smile. "So, what did you talk about?"

"I already told you."

"In detail, Ella. What specifically did you talk about? And why wouldn't you just come to me? You know, for this to work, you need to start talking to me about things. You used to talk to me about everything."

"That was before you…" Her mouth snaps closed. She doesn't need to finish the sentence. I already know what she was going to say.

"Before I left you." I nod, understanding.

"So, did you tell him how good I am at it at least?" I joke, trying to lighten the mood.

"No, that part must have skipped my memory."

"I'll be happy to refresh your memory, soon. First, I wanna know what exactly it was you talked about."

"You're not going to give up on this are you?" she asks, resigned.

"Nope." It's important I make her talk to me about this, even if she doesn't want to. It's like a band-aid — you just have to rip it off to realise it was way worse in your head. I need to get Ella out of her own head. I know she's scared to open up to me, because she thinks I'm going to leave.

"Okay, I asked him if what I like was normal," she says quietly.

I tilt my head at her. What she likes? "What do you mean? Is there something you like that I'm not doing? Because I'm pretty much open to anything you want to try in the bedroom. I only have a few hard limits." I wink at her.

"No, it's not that. I just… I like pain, Dean. I like it when you bite me, choke me, all of that. That's not normal, right? Bray says it is, but how can it be normal? I understand if you think I'm weird or whatever. But I've come to the conclusion that I don't care."

"First. Bray's right. It's completely normal. Besides, I like doing those things to you too. Second, you don't care about what, exactly?"

"I don't care if you try to leave me again." She shrugs her shoulders before smiling sweetly at me and adding, "I'll find a way to lock you in the basement of that big fancy house of yours. I'd keep you locked there forever if that's the only way I got to keep you."

I laugh so much my stomach starts to hurt. "And I'm unhinged?"

"Are you laughing at me, Dean?" Ella puffs out.

"No! I'd never dare to," I try to say with as straight a face as I can muster.

"I would hate for you to encounter an unfortunate accident," she threatens.

"Babe, you're not going to do anything to harm this body. You like it way too much." I'm pretty confident in that fact.

"Maybe?" She smiles and continues to dig into her food. I don't mind so much that she went to Bray about this stuff. But I sure as fuck want to be the one she comes to in the future.

"Ella?"

"Yeah?"

"I wish you had talked to me about this first," I say quietly.

"I was afraid that you would think I was weird or something…" Ella stares down at her plate.

"Babe, look at me," I command, my voice leaving no room for argument.

When she looks up from her plate, I tell her, "There is nothing weird about you. There is nothing about you that I don't love. Who the fuck cares if you like a little bit of pain with your pleasure? It's more normal and mainstream than you think."

"Yeah, but I don't have a normal relationship with pain, Dean. What if I'm using that as a way to get my fix?"

Shit, I didn't even really think of that connection. No wonder she's so worried about it.

"Does it feel the same? When you experience pain during an orgasm and when you cut?" I ask.

"No. At first I thought it was. But then, when I…" She pauses and a blank look takes over her features.

I stand up and walk around to her. Picking her up, I sit on the chair with her in my arms. "Go on," I encourage her.

"When I… when I cut today, it wasn't the same. It didn't feel the same," she says.

"Okay, that's good. Right?"

"I think so."

"Do you want me to get a therapist on the phone? We could do a consult over the phone right now if you want."

"Dean, it's eight o'clock at night. I can wait until we are back in Sydney. I'll call my therapist from Melbourne. I haven't found one in Sydney yet."

"Okay, but if you want one now, I can do that."

Ella leans into me, her lips connecting with mine. Her tongue pushes past my lips and entwines with mine. The sweet taste of her wine on her tongue makes me hungry for more. More of her. More of us. I pick her up and carry her inside. Laying her on the bed, I break apart the kiss.

"It's your birthday, Princess. Whatever you want, I'll do it. Tell me what you want?"

Chapter Nineteen

Ella

"ANYTHING I WANT, HUH?" I tap my finger on my chin, thinking of what I could possibly use this *anything I want* moment for. I must take too long thinking. Dean leans into my neck, kissing his way up to my ear.

"So, what'll it be? My tongue on that delicious pussy of yours. My fingers pumping in and out of that tight cunt I cannot stop fucking thinking about?"

I'm already a squirming, moaning mess. He's barely even touched me yet. But his words, oh, they've touched me. They have lit me up from the inside out.

"Or I could take your ass. That tight virgin ass." A growl leaves his throat. I can feel the vibrations of it on my neck.

I guess he likes the idea of fucking my ass. Me, not

so much. I need to put a stop to this before he seduces me into letting him do just that.

"I know what I want," I declare, my voice a breathy sigh.

"Yeah, what'll it be, Princess?"

"I want you to strip for me." My cheeks burn with embarrassment. But I want to see Dean strip.

"Okay, sure." He stands up, eyebrows drawn in confusion, as he starts to pull his shirt over his head.

"Wait, stop!" I hold my hand out in a stop motion.

"What?"

"Not like that. You need music. I want to see you dance while you do it. I want a show, Dean."

"You want a show?" His mouth hanging open, he scrubs a hand down the back of his neck. "Ah, babe. You know when I said you could have anything, I was kind of thinking: position, toy, body parts. Not dancing."

"Oh, well, that's okay," I say in a quiet voice. He immediately looks relieved.

"I mean, Magic Men are performing in Sydney in a few weeks. I'm sure Reilly will go with me." I shrug like it's not a big deal.

"Fuck no! You are out of your goddamn mind if you think you're going to watch a bunch of naked guys dance and gyrate. Not happening." Dean is fuming at the idea, exactly the reaction I knew he would have.

"I wasn't asking permission, Dean. I'm not your child, although you are basically old enough to be my dad. Well, if you can't give me a strip show, I'll go and see the professionals do it. It's not a big deal." I look him dead in the eye. I work hard on evening out my breathing. I'm the worst liar. I have no plans to go see a strip show. But I don't want him to know that.

"First, I'm ten years older than you, babe. I am not old enough to be your father. Although, I could be your *daddy*." He wags his eyebrows up and down.

I laugh at the thought, but some part deep inside me is kind of on board with that idea too. That's something I'll need to explore another time. One battle at a time.

"And second?" I ask.

"Okay, if I do this, you have to promise me you won't go to a fucking strip show."

"I promise." I jump up and down on the bed in excitement.

"I can't believe I'm fucking doing this. Only you could make me do this, Ella," Dean says as he thumbs through his phone. A smirk appears on his face as he hits play.

Ginuwine's "Pony" starts blasting from the phone's speaker. Oh. My. God. My hands are itching to pick up my phone and capture this on camera.

Dean starts to slowly move his hips, as his hands travel up and down his body and his chest, his movements a little awkward. The awkwardness does not last long though.

Grabbing his shirt between his hands, he rips the fabric straight down the middle, as he rolls his body.

My mouth hangs open as he begins a full-on choreo-graphed number.

He comes over and picks me up then settles me in a dining chair. I reach my hands up to touch his chest.

Dean swats my hands away. "No touching the talent." He winks and then starts giving me a lap dance. He's so fucking good at this, it's actually starting to piss me off. Has he done this before?

My thoughts are distracted by his abs though, before he flips himself upside down into some sort of handstand maneuver, his pelvis now gyrating near my face. I have to sit on my hands to stop myself from reaching out.

Why didn't I know he could dance? I feel like there is so much I don't know about him.

Dean rights himself and comes to straddle me again. His face goes into my neck, his chest heaving. The song's finished, which means my show is now finished. I've already decided this is so not going to be the last time he dances for me.

Dean slides his body down mine, until he is on his knees in front of me. He spreads my thighs apart as far as they will go. I don't get any warning before his face is buried between them, his tongue weaving magic over my body.

"Oh god! That, I want that now." I pant as I grab hold of his head, pushing his face harder into my core.

Dean doesn't complain. He lets out a guttural roar as his tongue plunges in and out of my pussy. Dean hooks his arms underneath my thighs, lifting my pelvis off the chair, and giving himself a better angle. His fingers are digging, bruising, into my thighs.

"Oh, fuck me!" I yell out. Dean pops his head up with a smirk.

"Don't worry, babe, I fully intend to."

"What the hell, Dean? Don't stop." I shamelessly shove his face back down into my pussy.

My whole body seizes and I come apart when he uses his fingernails to scratch into the sensitive skin of my upper thighs. I don't know what I'm yelling out, but I do know I'm making some incoherent sounds right now.

I must black out, because when I come to, I'm in the middle of the bed. *Naked.* Dean is straddling my body, naked as well, and smirking down at me. His ocean blue eyes are sparkling.

When I attempt to reach up to his face, my arms are met with restriction. I pull with no luck. Looking up, I see both wrists securely tied together with a silk tie, which is then fastened to the middle of the headboard. What the actual fuck? I thought he was joking about tying me to the bed.

I yank on my wrists again; the tie won't budge. Looking back at Dean, who still has a shit-eating grin on his face, I try to settle my racing heart. This is Dean. I trust Dean. I can handle being tied up and defenceless with Dean.

Dean tilts his head, inspecting my every reaction to my current predicament. His fingertips lightly graze down my body, from my neck to the middle of my breast. My skin erupts in goosebumps. A hot blaze follows his touch.

He trails his fingertips around both of my nipples, pinching, pulling, and twisting them at the same time. My back arches off the bed, the sensations going straight down to my core. I try to move my pelvis, looking for any kind of friction I can get. I don't get far. My legs are pinned down.

I'm literally held captive, my body at his mercy. And I'm absolutely loving it. In a matter of minutes, I've gone from scared to crazily wanton.

"Dean, please," I beg. Although I don't know what it is I'm begging for.

"Please what? What do you want, Ella?" his raspy voice asks.

"I want you to touch me," I manage to get out.

Dean's fingers leave my breast and start trailing in swirls around the sides of my waist. "I *am* touching you, babe."

My head shakes no. He is not touching me where I need to be touched. As soon as I make the motion, his fingers leave my body.

"No, you want me to stop?" he asks with a chuckle.

If I could send daggers with my eyes, they'd be going straight into him right now. "Don't you dare fucking stop."

"Tsk, tsk, tsk. You know that little potty mouth of

yours is going to get you in trouble. I think it needs to be cleansed out."

Dean shuffles up the length of my body, until he's squatting over my chest. He's holding his cock in his hand, stroking it up and down slowly. My mouth waters at the sight. Pre-cum glistens the tip.

My tongue darts out to lick my lips. Dean grunts as he rubs the tip of his cock along the seam of them. "Open," he demands.

I don't hesitate as my mouth opens and he glides his cock in as far as I can manage it. I flick my tongue up and down the underside of his cock, the smooth velvety skin a welcomed texture. The tangy, salty taste of him makes me thirsty for more.

"Suck, little girl. This is what happens to little girls who have potty mouths." He smirks.

I hollow my cheeks out and suck. Dean slowly begins to slide in and out of my mouth with long drawn-out movements.

"Fuck, Ella, your mouth feels so fucking good." He curses as he gradually picks up his speed.

"Mmmm," I moan around him. I'm so turned on and wet right now. My hips move on their own, seeking something. No, not something. My body is a greedy bitch, because it wants Dean's cock filling every hole.

Dean takes his cock out — a plop sound audible in the air — his movements so fast. One minute, he's squatting over my chest with his cock in my mouth. The next, he has my body flipped over. He positions me up on my knees so my ass is in the air and his cock is slamming into my pussy.

I'm so wet he glides in easily. Although it still takes a while for my body to adjust to the intrusion, I love the feel of him stretching me out. I love the slight tinge of pain as he fills me.

"You're so wet, hot, tight. I'm going to fuck you so goddamn hard you'll feel it in every fucking step you take tomorrow." He growls as he starts to do just that.

"Ahh, yes! Fuck! Oh god!" My mind is a mess, my body overcome with sensations. We haven't done this position before, the depths he is hitting inside me all new. Goddamn, what else has he been holding out on me? I know it's not a rational thought. I literally just had sex for the first time yesterday.

I can feel his hands everywhere, all over me. He pulls his cock out. I let out a whimper. Looking back over my shoulder, the best I can in this position, I watch as he gives me a devilish smirk while he inserts two fingers into my pussy. As quickly as he puts them in, he pulls them out.

He holds them up in front of his face, and I can see them glisten with my juices. My head falls back down to the mattress when he slams his cock into me again. He thrusts in and out, slowly. One of his hands comes around underneath me and starts rubbing circles around my clit.

His other hand lands on my ass with a loud smack. "Ah, fuck. God." I let out a mixture of curses and moans as the sting turns to pleasure. I want that again.

"Do that again," I beg.

"Gladly," he says at the same time his hand rains down on my ass. Three times. Each time a little harder than the first, and each time, that delicious sting sending waves of pleasure through my body.

I tense when I feel something moving around that forbidden little hole. No, he can't seriously think he's sticking anything in that.

"Relax, Princess. There is not a single part of this body that's not mine. That I won't treasure. That I won't pleasure." His words send shivers up and down my spine. He curves his body over mine and assaults my spine with feather-light kisses. He then finds a spot on the left side of my body, and bites down on my waist.

Intense pain radiates through me. Just as that pain is morphing into that wonderful bliss, I feel one finger slide into my rear hole. Fuck. His cock pumping in and out slowly, his fingers rubbing slow circles around my clit, and now my rear hole filled with a finger, he is keeping still.

I want more. I feel so full, so full of him. My hips grind back onto him. He gets the hint and picks up his pace. He begins fucking my pussy with his cock and my ass with his finger. It's not long before I'm drifting over the cliff.

I hear him call out my name as he comes, filling me up with his seed. After a minute, he leans over the top of me and loosens the ties around my wrists. We collapse on the bed next to each other, our breathing heavy. Dean has my wrists in his hands, rubbing over the marks left behind from the tie.

"Where on earth did you learn to do that?" I ask with a yawn.

He looks at me like I've grown two heads. "Ah, babe, you really want me to answer that?"

"Yes, I want to know."

"Well, I've been doing it ever since Miss Brighten. She was my year nine English teacher. Let's just say, she added an extra element to after school tutoring." He smirks.

"Your English teacher taught you how to dance?" I ask, confused. The look on his face tells me we are not talking about the same thing.

"Ah, not exactly," he answers as he looks up to the ceiling.

"Oh my god! Dean, you slept with your teacher?" I'm mortified. I mean, who actually does that?

"Well, yeah," he answers with a shrug. "Doesn't everyone?"

"No, Dean, everyone does not sleep with their teachers. I clearly never did."

"Please, your teachers weren't stupid enough to touch you, Ella. Trust me, they wanted to."

"No, they did not." There is no way that any of my teachers wanted to do anything like that with me.

"Babe, there is not a straight man alive that wouldn't want to get into your panties. They'll just never get to. Because. This. Is. Mine." He annunciates his claim slowly, firmly, as he cups his hand over my bare pussy.

"Uh-huh, all yours. Only yours. But I still wanna know. Where did you learn to dance like that?"

"My mother made us take dance lessons all through our childhood. When I was thirteen, I bribed the ballroom dance teacher to cover for us. Instead of the ballroom lessons my mother was paying for, we were learning hip hop."

He says this like it's totally normal for a thirteen-year-old to be bribing grown adults. Then my mind clicks on the *we* and the *us* he mentioned.

"Who's we?" I ask.

"Me and my brother."

"Wait. You have a brother?" I sit up fully now. "How do I not know you have a brother?"

"Josh. He's two years younger than me. Spends most of his time out on the family horse stud. He's also the CEO for McKinley Industries."

"Okay, well, I want to meet him."

"Sure, one day." He doesn't sound too convincing, like he wants me to meet his brother. I would dig into that further, but I'm too damn tired.

Lying back down, I rest my head on his chest. Placing a little kiss over his heart, I say, "I love you, Dean, so much it scares me. Because if I lose you again, I won't just be broken, I'll be fucking shattered into a million pieces."

"Ella, you're not going to lose me. I'm not going

anywhere. In fact, when we get back to Sydney, anywhere you go, I go. I'm not leaving your side for a second. It might be a good idea to work from home for a bit too."

"I'm not hiding from her, Dean. If she wants to come at me, let her." I will not be run out of my own club. Well, technically, it's Zac's club, but that's a minor detail.

"It's not hiding. If I don't think it's safe for you to be at the club, you won't be at the fucking club, Ella. I will not take risks when it comes to you."

"We can talk about this later. I'm tired." I yawn.

"Sure, Princess. Go to sleep." He kisses the top of my head, while tightening the arm that's draped around my waist and anchoring my body to his.

Chapter Twenty

Dean

THE WEEKEND WENT by way too fast for my liking.
I can't help but shake the feeling of dread in the pit of
my stomach. Something isn't right. The fact that we
are flying back into Sydney, back to where there is
currently a psycho sending threats to my girl… That
shit's not sitting well with me.

Every fibre of my being is telling me to direct this
plane elsewhere. To take Ella somewhere else. To find
a tower and hide her away from anyone who wants to
harm her. I can't do that though. If I'm not in Sydney,
I can't find the bitch and kill her myself.

Unfortunately for her, I know exactly who she is.
Where she lives. Where the fuck she works. There is
no rock she can fucking hide under that I will not turn
upside down. I'm going to enjoy getting her blood on
my hands.

We're all getting settled on the plane when Reilly asks Alyssa, "Hey, Lyssa, did you know Sarah was going away with that new guy of hers?"

"Yeah, she mentioned something to me last night about that," Alyssa answers.

I feel Ella go stiff next to me. I squeeze her hand and guide her to the back of the plane. She sits on the bed. Squatting down in front of her, I grasp both of her hands. "It's going to be okay, Ella. I won't let anyone get to you."

At that moment, Bray barges through the door. That fucker never fucking knocks.

"El, you doin' all right?" he asks her while leaning against the wall and making himself comfortable.

"I will be, Bray. I just... I don't know. It's not that I'm scared for myself. It's just... this is going to destroy Alyssa."

It's that moment that Zac decides to enter the room. What is it with Williamsons and not fucking knocking?

"What the fuck is going to destroy Alyssa?" he growls. He looks ready to murder someone.

Ella looks up to me and then to Bray. She doesn't want to say it. She can't bring herself to actually admit this to him.

"We know who's been taking the money from the club. We know who's been sending the threats to Ella," I tell him.

"Threats? As in there's been more than one?" he asks.

"Someone sent her a message yesterday over the club's servers. Dean was able to trace it. But Ella already knew who it was… The person is not happy that she's discovered their dirty little secret," Bray says between gritted teeth.

"Fuck! Why the fuck didn't you tell me this yesterday?"

"I… I had… I didn't want to ruin your weekend. I don't want this to be true. Why would they steal from you guys? I just don't get it. It doesn't make sense to me. But all the evidence is there."

"Who is it, El? Trust me when I say this. Whoever this fucker is, they will not live long enough to see any of their threats through. I will not let anyone hurt you."

"It's Sarah," Ella whispers with silent tears running down her face.

I watch as realisation dawns on Zac… as he grasps what this means for him and Alyssa. Sarah is his wife's best friend.

"How long has she been working at the club for anyway?" Ella asks him.

"She started a little over a year ago. She needed extra money so we gave her bartending gigs. She worked her way up to managing the bar," I tell her.

"Okay, this is what's going to happen. Not a word of this to Alyssa yet. I'll figure out how to tell her. We don't know where she is right now. She's desperate, which means she's dangerous." Zac paces around the small room.

"Dean, Reilly and I need a place to crash for a few weeks. Think you can spare a few rooms in that little house of yours?" Bray asks.

"What's wrong with your house?" Ella queries. I smile. I know exactly what he's up to.

"Sure thing, man. I'll send a text and have a room set up for the girls too."

"Thanks. My house is getting some work done to it. I don't want the construction work to upset the girls' routine," he replies, answering Ella's question. He then looks directly at me. "Don't go fucking overboard on setting up a room for Hope and Lily. They're babies, Dean. They don't need much."

I just shrug. If I want them to have a room fit for the princesses they are while they are in my house, then that's exactly what they'll have.

"Think we should get them a couple of ponies while they are with us, babe?" I ask Ella.

She laughs while Bray vetoes the idea.

"Oh, shit. I just remembered. You said Alyssa and I could stay at your house this week while ours was being painted," Zac says.

"Fuck, I forgot about that. It's fine. You can have your usual room, and Ash is already set up there."

"Thanks. He'll be thrilled. He loves staying at your place."

I honestly don't know how Ella did not inherit the lying abilities that her brothers have. They both managed to come up with that shit quick. Even though I know they are both full of shit, Ella is none the wiser.

"Maybe I should just stay at the penthouse this week, Dean. Sounds like you're going to have your house full anyway."

"*We* are going to have our house full, Ella. You're not leaving your home just because your idiot brothers decided to both do home renos in the same week. Besides, our house is big enough that you'll barely notice they are there."

She looks between the two of them, both standing stoic with their arms crossed over their chests. "That's doubtful," she says with a smile when she looks back at me.

"Okay, let's get home. Not a word of this to Alyssa until we figure out how we're going to handle this." Zac points at all three of us.

"Sure," Bray and I say at the same time, while Ella nods her head in agreement.

"Zac, wait up, man," I say, wanting to talk to him alone. I kiss Ella on her forehead. "I'll meet you out there in a sec. Save me a seat."

"Okay."

"Babe, make sure it's far away from Bray," I call out as she's walking out the door. I hear Ella giggle and Bray curse under his breath.

Once they're both out the door, I close it behind them. I turn around and head for the cabinet where I know there's a bottle of whisky. I pour two glasses, handing one to Zac.

He downs it in one go. He's struggling to rein it in right now. I can tell.

"You aren't doing this one, Zac," I tell him as I refill his glass.

"What do you mean I'm not doing this one? That bitch is threatening Ella. Not only am I going to do this, I'm going to fucking do it with a goddamn smile on my face."

"No doubt. But how do you think you're going to face Alyssa afterwards, knowing you killed her best friend?"

That wipes the confidence off his face. "Fuck! This shit is going to fucking hurt her, man. She loves Sarah like a fucking sister. Why wouldn't she just come to me if she needed money?"

"Because your warm, cuddly, welcoming personality just screams at people to come ask you for money. Sure, man."

Zac sits on the bed and runs his hands through his hair. He's probably not going to like what I've got to tell him next either. I just need to do it, rip the band-aid off. It's happening whether he likes it or not anyway.

"I'm going to marry Ella," I blurt out fast. I know I don't need his approval, but I'd still like him to be with me on this, not against it.

He smirks at me. "Does she know about this?" he asks.

"We've talked about it. I haven't exactly asked her yet. She also doesn't know it's happening sooner rather than later," I admit.

"How soon are we talking, Dean?"

"The papers will be waiting when we get home. All we have to do is sign them."

"Fuck no! I get that you want to marry her, but fuck, man. You can't do it like that. She deserves a fucking proper wedding. A white dress and all that shit."

"I know. And she will get that, as soon as this shit is settled. But right now, I need to make her a McKinley. I called Josh."

"Why the fuck would you call him? We don't need his kind of fucking crazy, Dean. We can handle this shit ourselves." He curses as he gets up and starts pacing the room.

"Because this is Ella, Zac. I'm not taking any fucking chances. I will use whatever resource I have in my arsenal to make sure she's safe."

He knows I'm right. He knows that we need to do everything we can to make sure Ella is safe.

"Okay, so what's the plan? I know you got one." Zac raises an eyebrow at me in question.

"I'm taking Ella out to the stud farm. We're going to draw Sarah out there. All you need to do is get Alyssa or Reilly to let it slip that Ella and I are staying at the farm for a few weeks. You won't have to know the details. You don't need to be involved in this, Zac. I will make sure she's never seen again."

"Josh still got the pigs?"

I laugh. My crazy-ass brother makes all of us look

like fucking choir boys. "Yeah, that fuckers attached to those things. Treats them like his damn kids."

"Let's hope he never actually breeds and has human kids then."

"Not sure there's a woman alive stupid enough to breed with him. Come on, let's get out there so we can get home."

Walking into the kitchen, I find Ella showing Alyssa how to operate the coffee machine. I'm not really sure why. I don't think I've ever seen Alyssa make her own coffee.

"Princess, you know we have staff for that, right? Alyssa, if you need anything while you're here, just talk to Geoffrey. He'll make sure you get it." Geoffrey has been with the family for longer than I can remember. It still amazes me, the things he is able to get his hands on at short notice.

"Oh, I also asked Beth to check with you on what Ash eats. She's going to need a grocery list and a menu," I tell Alyssa, who looks at me like I have suddenly grown two heads.

"Who's Beth? And seriously, a menu? Dean, we

don't need to be catered for. I'm more than capable of cooking and cleaning and all of that. This isn't a vacation. I didn't even know Zac arranged for the house to be painted until today."

"I know you're capable, Lyssa. It's Beth's job to cook for the household. It's her livelihood, Lyssa. She takes great pride in what she does here. Don't take that away from her. Humour her for me and give her a menu fit for a prince."

"Well, shit. When you put it like that, Dean, okay, I'll give her some ideas," Alyssa relents. Thank God, I did not want Alyssa and Reilly messing around in my kitchen.

"Great. Thank you. Ella, I need to show you something." I take her hand and lead her out of the kitchen.

"What is it?" Ella asks.

"You'll see," I reply. Then I remember the whole not great with surprises chat we've already had.

"It's your birthday gift. I bought you a house. But I'm not telling you where. That part you will have to trust me with and let me take you there." I've stopped us in the garage.

"What do you mean you bought me a house? Dean, people don't go around buying their girlfriends houses for their birthday. That's too much," she protests.

"Babe. Do you want to see the house?" I ask.

"Shut up. Of course, I want to see the house! I can't believe you bought me a house. You know, even if it's a Barbie dream house, I'll be thrilled," she says.

"Uh-huh, I think you'll like this one more than a Barbie dream house, babe. Which car?" I ask her.

This makes her take in her surroundings. She hasn't been in the garage yet, hasn't seen the stupid collection of cars that are in here. Most of these cars were obtained by my father; he had a penchant for flaunting his money. I prefer to fly under the radar. But there are a few in here that I've splashed out on.

"Um, Dean, what the hell? This is nuts." Ella waves her hand around the garage. She starts to stroll through, weaving in and out of cars, before stopping at a white Maserati MC20. I smile. That baby is my newest purchase, drives like a fucking dream.

"This one." Ella runs her hand down the side of the car. I inwardly cringe at the idea of her handprints being left behind on the otherwise meticulously clean surface.

I find the key fob on the wall. "Okay, let's go."

As we're driving out of the estate, Ella is examining every little detail of the car. She grew up with Zac, so she knows her cars well.

"Does Zac know you have this?" she asks.

I laugh. Zac's wanted one of these since he heard they were being released. I just happened to have the first one in Australia. He doesn't know yet. Like I said, I don't flaunt my wealth. "No, he hasn't seen it yet."

"Well, that explains why it's still in your garage and not his then."

She adjusts the volume of the music. Some god-awful sounds scream from the speakers. I turn it down slightly. "El, I love you… but your taste in music fucking sucks," I tell her, grabbing hold of her hand.

"Yeah, well, your taste in…" She looks me up and down, trying her hardest to think of a comeback. "I don't know what yet. But whatever it is, it sucks."

The rest of the drive to Palm Beach is spent with us laughing and being carefree. As we pull onto the street the house is on, I tell her to close her eyes. To my surprise, she actually does.

"Don't open them until I tell you to." Jumping out of the car, I jog around to her side and open her door. "Keep them closed," I whisper in her ear as I lean over to unbuckle her seatbelt. Holding onto both of her hands, I help her out of the car and guide her until she is standing in the middle of the driveway.

Standing behind her, with my arms wrapped around her waist, I run my tongue up the side of her neck. "You're such a good girl, Ella, keeping your eyes closed all this time. Good things happen to good girls." I trail my hand under her skirt, heading straight to my promised land. Her body shivers. I didn't miss the way her body sank into mine, the little sigh she let out at being told she was a good girl. I'm going to have to explore that a little more.

Ella moans. I wasn't planning this. But I can't seem to help myself where she's concerned. With each touch, each taste, I crave more. My fingers push aside her panties, rubbing circles around her clit. Her little whimpers and moans sooth my soul. I'll never tire of seeing Ella in the throes of pleasure.

"I'm going to give my good girl a little treat before her surprise," I tell her and watch as her body quakes, her knees buckling beneath me. I nibble lightly on her neck, grazing the skin with my teeth and teasing her with the promise of that bite that she's craving.

"I think you like being my good little girl. Do you, Princess? Do you want to be my good girl?" I ask her.

Ella groans as she pushes her pussy harder down onto my hand. "Yes." She says the single word, confirming my suspicions.

"We are going to have so much fun exploring this new little development, Princess." I thrust two fingers inside of her. My cock is fucking aching in my pants, desperate to replace my fingers and fill her up.

"Right now, I need you to be really good and come for me. I need you to be my good girl and come right now, Princess." I feel her body tense up. Her pussy tightens and clamps down on my fingers. She's trying to be quiet, unsuccessfully. Her juices drip down my hand.

Pulling my fingers out, I bring them to my mouth and lick them clean. Her taste is the sweetest of any treat I've ever had.

"Open your eyes, Ella. Happy Birthday."

Chapter Twenty-One

Ella

I OPEN MY EYES; my mind is still fog-induced from the orgasm Dean just sprung on me. Not that I'm complaining — I'll take them as often as he wants to hand them out.

My eyes focus in on what it is I'm standing in front of. It's a house. A large white house with blue trimmings around the awnings and windows. I honestly thought he was kidding about the whole *I bought you a house* thing.

"Uh, Dean, this is a house. Whose is it?" I ask. We are standing in the driveway of a house and he just finger-banged me. Here, out in the open, for anyone to see.

"It's yours. Come on inside and have a look." Dean tugs on my hand, leading me to the front door.

He opens the door and walks straight in. I stop in

the foyer. This isn't just a house; this is fucking huge! Stunning. I turn in a circle, trying to take as much in as I can. There's a staircase off to the left-hand side of the foyer. The space is open, a wide hall leading you into other rooms. I can see three doorways along the hall and a larger opening at the end.

"I thought you were kidding, Dean. You can't seriously buy me a house. This is too much."

"Come on, you haven't even seen the best bit yet."

I follow him through the hall. We end up in a large open-space living area. There's a galley style kitchen with timber benchtops and white cabinets to one side. But it's the floor-to-ceiling windows that have captured my attention.

I head straight for them. There's a large sliding door that leads onto a deck. Opening the door, I'm assaulted with the smell and sounds of the ocean. This house is on the beach. Literally. The deck I'm standing on leads to the sand.

I know this beach. Looking up and down the familiar beach, I hardly notice as Dean's arms come and wrap around my shoulders from behind me, pulling me up against his chest.

"Do you like it?" he asks tentatively.

"Ah, this is Palm Beach, Dean," I say.

"Yeah, I know. What do you think of the house?"

"The house is gorgeous, but it's way too much. You can't buy this for a birthday present." I shake my head. Who buys someone a house for their birthday?

"I can and I have. It's yours. It's already done."

I pull out of his arms and turn around to face him. "Did you buy me a house because you want me out of yours?" I question, my stomach doing backflips.

"What? NO!" Dean reaches for me but I step back.

"Ella, no. I bought you a beach house because it's been your dream to have one ever since I've known you. I bought this house so we could spend weekends here, *together.* But I guess if you want to live here full-time, then we can move in here. The closet space isn't as big though."

"You bought a house on Palm Beach as a week-ender? Dean, that's crazy expensive."

He just shrugs. "Come on, there's something upstairs I want to show you."

I hope it's a bed. Actually I don't even need a bed. I'll settle for a wall, a bench, the floor. As long as it ends up with his cock inside me. The moan I thought was only in my head must have come out loud, because Dean turns his head back to me and smirks.

He leads me up the stairs and to a doorway. We end up in what must be the master bedroom. There's no bed. The otherwise empty room is, however, decorated with flowers, red roses everywhere and candles. Standing in the middle of the room, I'm lost for words. It's beautiful.

"Ella, I know you deserve so much more than this." Dean gets down on one knee in front of me. He holds both my now shaking hands in his.

"Ella, you are my everything. I want to wake up next to you every day. I want to create a lifetime of memories with you. I will always put you first, above anything and anyone else. Ella, will you marry me?"

Reaching into his pocket, he pulls out a ring and holds it up to my finger. He looks up at me, waiting for my answer. I nod my head.

"Yes," I whisper, before I jump on him. He falls back. I don't care though; my mouth is finding his before he even has time to put that ring on my finger. Our tongues mash together.

Dean pulls on my hair, breaking our kiss apart. "As much as I'm enjoying being mauled by you right now, Princess, I've been waiting a really fucking long time to put this ring on your finger."

I hold my hand up and he slips the rock on my finger. It's a huge princess-cut solitaire diamond. I fucking love it. "It's beautiful, Dean. Thank you."

"Babe, it's me that should be thanking you. You just made me the happiest fucking man around."

Dean sits up, holding me to his body. My legs wrap around his waist. "I can't believe this is happening. This is real, isn't it? It's not a dream?" I ask.

"It's a dream for sure, Princess, but very, very real. This is happening. You are going to be my wife. Actually, about that, I have to run something by you."

"Okay, if this is the part where you tell me you have other wives, and I'm going to be a sister wife, you can forget it. I'll kill them and have Bray help me bury the bodies." I give him my sweetest smile.

"Ah, no. Trust me, El, you are the only girl for me. Always have. Always will."

"Okay, good answer. What is it then?"

"Just know that I plan to make sure you have your dream wedding, with the white dress, the cake, the party, all that jazz. But I have papers sitting on my desk at home. I want us to sign the papers tonight. I want you to marry me tonight. And then we can plan the wedding, the honeymoon. Everything."

He wants to marry me tonight? On paper. "Why?" I ask. Why does he need me to sign papers tonight, to be married tonight?

"I want you to be my wife. I don't want to wait."

"Okay. On one condition."

"Name it. Anything you want, it's already yours," he says while rubbing his hands up and down my thighs.

"I want to drive that fancy car of yours back home." I smile.

Dean groans. "Ah, babe, are you sure that's what you want? You could have anything." He tries to talk me out of wanting to drive.

I laugh. "I'm sure. Now let's go. I want to drive that thing."

"Okay. But, Ella, seriously, I love you and all. But do not hurt my damn car." Dean looks stressed as he says this.

I practically run out to the car.

"Oh my god! We have to do this again. I love this thing!" I scream as we come to a stop out front of Dean's house. Dean looks a little green at the moment.

"Never again! How did you even pass a driver's test, El?"

"What? I'm a perfectly good driver. You're still in one piece, aren't you?" My arms fold over my chest.

"No, I think I left half my insides at that first red light you ran." He opens his door and starts walking around my side of the car. I don't wait for him this time. Before he can get to my door, I'm out of the car and slamming the door, which only makes him cringe.

"It was orange, not red!" I yell.

"I'm not colour-blind, babe. It was red. I'm probably going to have at least ten speeding fines coming in the mail too. How is it I've never actually seen you drive before?"

"Oh, I don't know, probably because I'm surrounded by alpha-holes who always insist on driving me around." I throw my arms up in the air as I stomp towards the house.

The door flies open, Zac standing in the doorway. "What the fuck are you two yelling about out here?"

"Just the fact that your sister almost killed me! Have you seen her drive?" Dean yells back at him.

Zac smiles. "You let her drive?" Then his eyes land on the car. "What the fuck, D! You let her drive that? When the fuck did you even get this?" Zac's making his way to the car. Me? Apparently I'm forgotten about.

"Just last week. I'm lucky she's still in one piece." Dean shakes his head.

Deciding to leave them to it, I head for the door. "This conversation isn't over, Princess," Dean says. To which, I flip him off without even a look back at him.

Walking through the house, I look for Reilly or Alyssa—either of them will do. I just need to show someone this ring. I can't believe I'm actually going to be married. I'm going to marry Dean. The person I thought I'd never get to have, I get to have him forever.

My smile hurts my face, but I can't stop. I'm staring down at my hand as I'm walking. I don't notice my surroundings until it's too late. I walk straight into someone. Hands instantly grab my arms to steady me. I look up, about to apologise. The moment my eyes land on his face, my whole body freezes. I don't know this person. I've never seen him around here before. The emptiness in his eyes, staring back at me, sends chills down my spine.

I react on instinct. My knee comes up, connecting

with his nuts. This makes his hands fall from my arms. I take the opportunity of him being crunched over to grab hold of one of his arms and flip him onto his back.

"Fuck me!" he howls out. But instead of the angry expression and fight I'm expecting to receive from him, he stares up at me, a huge smile spread across his face.

"What the fuck are you smiling at?" I cross my arms over my chest.

He laughs as he says, "I take it you're Ella."

"Josh? What are you doing here? And what the fuck are you doing on the floor?" Dean questions, looking from me to this Josh guy.

"I'm here because it's not every day your brother gets married. I'm on the floor because, apparently, you're marrying fucking Harley Quinn," Josh says as he stands up, cupping his junk. "I approve by the way."

"Wasn't looking for your approval, asshole." Dean comes and stands in front of me. "Babe, did he do something to you?" Dean asks me.

"What? No." I shake my head.

"Then why'd you put him on his ass?"

"It was my fault. I wasn't looking where I was going. I walked into him and he grabbed my arms to stop me from falling." I step to the side so I can see Josh. I should apologise. What a way to make a good impression on Dean's family.

"I'm sorry. Do you want some, um… ice… or something?" I ask him, pointing to his junk.

"Don't apologise to him. This is your house. He shouldn't be lurking in the fucking shadows," Dean growls.

"It's okay, sweetheart. It's not the first time my balls have taken a knee. Probably won't be the last either," Josh says, totally ignoring Dean's comment.

"Her name is Ella, Josh. Not sweetheart," Dean grunts.

"I really am sorry. Let me get you a drink at least. Come on, I happen to know where he keeps the good stuff." I step around Dean and start towards the room I know there is a bar in. "Also don't worry about him; he's just grouchy because I'm a way better driver than he is," I add as Josh and I make our way to the bar.

"Okay, so I want all the juicy embarrassing stories — quick before he comes in and puts a stop to this," I say as I pour us both a shot of Dean's top-shelf whisky.

"Yeah, I'm actually a little shocked he let you walk in here with me alone. Although, the fucker probably has the place rigged with cameras everywhere." Josh looks up at the ceilings of the room.

"Oh, he does for sure. But you're his brother. Why wouldn't he let me walk into a room with you? You don't look that scary… and then there's the fact I already put you on your ass once. I can do it again."

"You caught me off guard. Trust me, sweetheart, it won't happen again. Don't be fooled by the good looks. I can be plenty dangerous when I need to be."

"Maybe." I pour us another shot each.

"Here's to new family and making memories," I toast as we click glasses together.

"You know, I think I'm gonna like having you around. Trust me when I say that's a compliment," Josh says. Reaching for the bottle, he pours our next shot. At this rate, I'm going to be smashed before I have a chance to sign those papers of Dean's.

"Well, too bad if you don't. Because I'm not going anywhere," I inform him.

He chuckles as he takes a sip of his whisky. Okay, I guess we're slowing down on the drinking. "So, sweetheart, what is a girl like you doing with a dope like my brother?"

"I happen to love that big dope very much. Plus, he's really, really good with his…" I'm interrupted by Bray's booming voice.

"For the love of God, Ella, do not finish that fucking sentence!"

"Tongue." I finish my sentence anyway. Bray groans as he comes and takes a seat at the bar.

"Family trait, I'm afraid," Josh says.

"I'll take your word for it."

"I have references — you want them?" Josh starts digging out his phone.

"Nope, I'm good. I do not need to see your DLBB, thank you very much."

"DLBB?" Josh raises his eyebrows in question.

"Your digital little black book." I grab the bottle of whisky from him and refill our glasses. I grab another glass out for Bray. Filling it, I hand it over.

"They send you in to babysit?" Josh asks him.

"No, but when I heard you were in here alone with her…" Bray points to me. "I was suddenly thirsty." He sips at his glass.

"Well, you don't need to worry. Ella and I are getting along like a house on fire. She is perfectly safe with me," Josh directs at Bray.

Bray squints his eyes at Josh, then asks me, "How much has he had to drink?"

"Not much. We were just getting started when you came in with your whole buzzkill attitude." I wave my hands around in front of his face.

Bray reaches out and grabs hold of my hand. "What the fuck is that?" he yells, dropping my hand like it's burned him.

Holding my hand up, I can't help but smile at the shiny rock. "Dean asked me to marry him," I squeal.

"And you said yes? Ella you're so young. You shouldn't rush into this." Bray gets up and starts yelling curse words and pacing. I'm about to apologise for Bray's antics. But when I look at Josh, I feel like I'm looking at a whole new person.

That empty icy glare is back in his eyes, his body tense. I watch dumbfounded, as he stands up and positions himself in front of me.

"You might want to stop yelling at her before I make it so you can't yell at all." Something in Josh's voice tells me he's not making empty threats.

"Fucking hell, I forgot just how crazy your ass is. She's my sister. If I want to yell some sense into her, I will." Bray keeps pacing up and down the room, not deterred by Josh's threats at all.

"Yeah, guess what?" Josh asks him in a calm tone. A very eerily calm tone.

"What?"

"She happens to be my sister now. And nobody yells at my sister and lives to tell the story. I don't care who you are." I need to step in here before these two idiots decide to take their pissing fight further.

"Okay, that's it. You're both ruining my buzz now." I jump on top of the bar, sit crossed-legged and pour another drink. This is the exact moment Dean and Zac decide to walk in.

Dean looks at Josh, then at Bray before asking me, "What's going on?"

"Well," I start, then hold up my hand, indicating for him to hold that thought. As I'm tossing my shot back, Josh answers for me.

"He seems to think it's okay to yell at Ella. Either one of you put a stop to it, or I will."

"What? Why the fuck are you yelling at her?" Dean asks Bray at the same time Zac walks over and smacks him upside the head.

"Leave her alone, idiot." Zac uses his *dad* voice on him.

"Are you seriously going to let her get married?" Bray asks Zac.

"She's fucking twenty-three, idiot. I'm not letting her do shit. If she wants to marry the idiot, that's her choice, not ours."

Chapter Twenty-Two

Dean

WHAT THE HELL IS HAPPENING? I walk into the room to find Ella sitting on the bar top with a bottle of whisky in her hands, my fucking psycho brother standing in front of her like he is her self-appointed bodyguard.

Bray's fucking pacing up and down the room not happy about something.

When Josh says Bray's been yelling at Ella, I have a feeling he's not too happy about the ring on her finger. My suspicions are confirmed when he starts yelling at Zac about letting her get married.

Because any of us let Ella *do* anything. That girl does what she wants, despite what anyone else thinks. I'll also be damned if any fucker is going to stop us from signing those papers tonight.

With that thought, I head over to the bar. "How

much have you had to drink, Princess?" I need her sober to sign these papers.

Ella holds the bottle up. "Not much?" she answers with a question.

Okay. We need coffee. Reaching over the other side of the bar, I pick up the phone and dial through to the kitchen. When Beth answers, I tell her to bring a pot of coffee in here. I pry the whiskey bottle out of Ella's hands, much to her annoyance.

"Hey, Joshy and I were bonding over that bottle." She pouts.

I glare at my brother. Joshy? Really. What the fuck did I miss?

"Princess, we have very important plans tonight. I need you to be sober for them."

Ella reaches up and wraps her arms around my neck, then brings her legs around my waist. "Do these plans involve your tongue? Because I was just saying how you can do good things with your tongue," she whispers harshly.

"Well, if you drink some coffee and sober up, babe, I can guarantee you that I'll make that happen," I promise her.

"Okay, where's the coffee?" she asks, poking her head around my shoulders.

"Did I miss the party invite?" Reilly heads over to Bray. I watch as his body relaxes the moment she wraps her arms around his neck.

"No," Bray says at the same time Ella holds her hand out and says, "Yes, look what I got!"

The sound that comes out of Reilly's mouth should be illegal. I'm not even sure what it is, but it's fucking high-pitched and goes straight through my bones.

"Babe, calm down. You're going to make us all deaf," Bray groans.

"I don't care! Let me see! Let me see!" Reilly jumps up and down as she pushes me to the side and pulls on Ella's hand.

Josh's features harden as he takes in Reilly tugging on Ella's hand. I give my head a slight shake. This is not something he wants to comment on. Instead, he speaks to Ella.

"Sweetheart, I think you should maybe hop down off the bar before your friend here pulls you down."

"Josh, this is Reilly. Reilly, Josh. She's my sister. For some reason, she married Bray." Ella sticks her tongue out pretending to gag.

"Oh, there's a reason — it's his pierced cucumber. That thing is bloody magic." Reilly laughs. At this, Bray's chest puffs out, and a smirk crosses his features.

Ella screws her face up. "Yuck, I do not need to know about that. Do you want to hear about Bray's cucumber?" she asks Josh.

"Fuck no."

"Well, let's get back to the fact that I'm getting married. Tonight." Ella jumps up and down in her spot. She's still on the bar.

"Either you get her down, or I will," Josh says to me. I'm already grabbing her by the waist and picking her up. I sit her on the barstool in front of her.

Beth walks into the room rolling a coffee cart. Her cart automatically stops when she spots Josh. She makes the sign of the cross with shaky hands as she mumbles a prayer under her breath.

Josh smirks at her, which she does not like one bit. She leaves the cart where she stands in the doorway, turns on her heel and walks away.

"What the hell did you do to that poor woman?" I ask Josh.

He smiles. "I think it's probably more what I did to her granddaughter."

"I think it's more that she knows the devil when she sees him," Bray counters.

"Probably," Josh says, unfazed by the comment as he walks over and pours Ella a cup of black coffee. He's about to bring the cup over when he looks at her, then adds milk before handing it to her.

"Thanks, Bro," Ella says as she takes the cup.

"Just so you know, you may be her new brother, but I'm her favourite brother," Bray says as he stalks up to Ella.

"El, if you're one hundred percent sure this is what you want to do, then I'm happy for you. But if there is the slightest doubt, let me know and I'll get you out of here."

Even though I don't doubt Ella's love, I still seem to hold my breath at Bray's question, waiting to hear her answer. She keeps me waiting a while too, damn it. As she slowly sips her coffee, she puts the cup down on the bench.

"Bray, I am one hundred percent certain. This is what I want. He is what I want," she says, pointing her thumb over her shoulder at me. I let out the breath I was holding, a huge smile plastered on my face.

"Okay, we'll be back. Let's meet in the ballroom in an hour." I pick Ella up off the barstool and steady her on her feet. She gets her balance pretty quickly. Maybe she's not as drunk as I thought.

"You have a ballroom? Seriously, Dean, who the hell has a ballroom in their house?" She shakes her head in disbelief.

"We do, babe."

As I'm leading her out of the room, I stop at Josh. "Don't kill anyone." I shouldn't have to tell my younger brother not to kill anyone, but it's Josh — you never know when his crazy ass is going to do something stupid.

"Sure thing. I'll be like Mother fucking Teresa." He salutes me.

"Holy shit, you really are good with that tongue." Ella pants and puffs as I kiss my way back up her body. I chuckle at the memory of the look on her brothers' faces when she mentioned that little fact to them.

"I'm good at a lot of things, Princess. Things I plan to show you, right after we're married tonight," I promise.

"Uh, Dean, I'm pretty sure it's a bit late for the whole waiting until marriage thing."

"Oh, I know it's too late for that. But we have to get out of this shower. We have somewhere to be."

"I can't wait to be your wife."

"Mmm, I can't wait to do unspeakable things to my wife." I nibble on her earlobe. I don't think I'll ever get tired of hearing her little moans of pleasure.

"I'm going to try, you know. I want to be the best wife you could ever dream of having."

"Ella, you don't have to try. You don't have to be anything that you're not already. I want you just the way you are. I wish you could see yourself through my eyes — you're fucking perfect, babe." It wrecks me that she thinks she's not perfect.

"I just don't want to disappoint you."

"You won't. I am crazily in love with you, Ella. No one else. Just you. You are the one who has my ring on your finger. You are the one who will be the mother to my children — if we decide to have any."

"I know you're getting on and all in age, but I

don't know if I want kids just yet. Maybe in a few years." Ella laughs.

"Sure, babe, I can wheel them around in the mobility scooter I'll be getting around in by next year."

The sound of Ella's laughter fills the room as we dry off and head for the closet. I had Alyssa find her a white dress. It's not a wedding dress, but it's at least white. It's draped over the island bench.

"I hope you don't mind, but I had Alyssa find you a white dress. I know this isn't ideal and it's not the way we should do this getting married thing. But it means the world to me that you're doing it this way. We will absolutely be having the wedding of your dreams." I kiss her forehead and pull her body tight against mine.

She wraps her arms around my waist. "Dean, I don't need a big fancy wedding. I don't need all the frills and whistles. I just need you."

"Okay, let's get dressed so I can put a ring on you."

"Let's."

Chapter Twenty-Three

Ella

I CANNOT BELIEVE I'm about to sign a piece of paper and be officially married to Dean. The dress that Alyssa found for me is beautiful. The top is fitted white satin and square cut, which makes my boobs pop up. The rest of the dress is chiffon fabric, which drapes over my curves. It's long, falling down past my feet. I love it. I forgo wearing shoes and opt to be barefoot. We are only walking down the hallway after all.

Leaving my hair out, and letting it fall down my back in thick waves, I put on some mascara and lip gloss and call it a day. As much as I want to make myself look my absolute best for Dean, I'm running out of time. Also, I'm just really anxious to be married to him already.

I know Dean thinks I need to have a big flashy

wedding with all the bells, but I don't. The fact that it's simple suits me just fine. I used to daydream about marrying him and what our life would be like together.

The reality of what it's like is so much better than anything I could have ever dreamt up. I get butterflies every time I see him still. I want to climb him like a tree every other second. I thought I'd be nervous when I got married. People make it out to be such a big deal.

Stepping out of the dressing room, I see that Dean's waiting for me as he leans against the dresser. His eyes slowly roam up and down my body. Not once, but three times. I'm suddenly nervous. Does he not like the dress? Did he expect me to get more done up?

"Fucking hell, you look fucking stunning, Ella." Dean walks over to me. "I can't even put into words how fucking amazing you look right now, Princess. I'm... you are beautiful."

"Thank you. You don't scrub up too bad your-self," I tell him.

Dean's wearing a pair of black slacks, a white shirt underneath his jacket with a grey tie. I know I see him in a suit every day at work. But damn, I can never see him dressed like this enough. Knowing what's under-neath the suit makes it all that much better.

As we walk through this museum Dean calls a house, my white dress flows around my legs. But all I feel is peace.

I'm calm. I'm grounded. I feel like I'm finally home. "Thank you," I tell Dean as we walk hand in hand towards the ballroom I didn't even know was here. This house is ridiculous. If it were up to me, we would be spending most of our time in that beach house he bought.

"What are you thanking me for?" Dean asks.

"For marrying me, for choosing me."

There was a long time I didn't think he would choose me. I thought this was completely one-sided. I've been infatuated with Dean for so long… it's hard to remember a time where I wasn't.

"No need to thank me, Princess — you're giving me everything I've always wanted. The one thing I thought I'd never get to have." Dean brings our joined hands up to his mouth and kisses each one of my knuckles.

"Ready?" he asks.

"Like you wouldn't believe." My smile is so big. I'm trying my hardest to contain my excitement. I don't want to be jumping up and down right now like a kid on Christmas, even if that's exactly what I feel like. A kid on Christmas, unwrapping everything that was on her list.

I'm so giddy with excitement that it's not until I'm almost to the middle of the room that I notice my surroundings. I stop on the spot, my mouth hanging open. I've never seen anything more beautiful. There are white flowers everywhere, and candles all around the room. White drapes hang low from the tall ceilings with fairy lights entwined around them.

"Oh my gosh, Dean! This is stunning." My voice chokes with emotion. In the middle of the room is a long dining table. My whole family is sitting around it, all staring at me.

The attention from everyone at once making me somewhat anxious, I withdraw a little and stand behind Dean slightly more. I spin around in a circle, taking in the rest of the room. When I make it back around, everyone is still staring at me.

My hands go to my wrist, trying to cover as much skin as I can. It's like they can all see my scars, even though I know I covered them.

"Princess? You good?" Dean asks.

"Uh, yeah. Of course." I plaster a smile on my face. Although by the squint of Dean's eyes, he can tell it's fake. I look beyond Dean, at everyone sitting at the table. This is my family. I shouldn't feel like this under their gaze. But I can't help it.

My eyes connect with Josh's. He looks pissed off. I don't know why. Is it me? Maybe he doesn't want Dean and me to get married.

"Okay, fuckers, let's eat. I'm starving," Josh says, breaking everyone's attention away from me. He then winks at me. I send a small smile of thanks to him as Dean leads me over to the table.

Once we're sitting, Dean takes hold of my hand. "Before we start, I just want to thank you all for being here. It means a lot to Ella and me that you're here for this moment."

In front of me is a pen and some papers. A tall, leggy blonde enters the room and Dean nods at her as she approaches the table. The way she smiles and licks her lips at Dean, yeah, I already don't like her — whoever the hell she is.

"Ella, this is Stephanie, our solicitor. She is here to witness the papers being signed." Dean introduces her, although she doesn't take her eyes off him.

"Hi." I smile politely. She still pays me no mind.

"How've you been?" She talks directly to Dean.

"Good, you?" Dean's answer is short, his tone sharp. Please, God, tell me he hasn't slept with his damn solicitor.

Something nudges my foot under the table. Across the table from me, Josh is smirking. I have no idea what he finds amusing right now.

Bray is sitting to my right; he leans down and whispers in my ear, "You doin' all right, El? Want me to wipe the smirk off the bastard's face?"

"I'm fine," I whisper back.

Dean's arm comes around my shoulders. I expect him to rest a hand on my shoulder, except he pulls my chair closer to him. His arm drops around my waist, his hand landing on top of my hand. It's not until he squeezes my hand that I realise I was gripping the knife. I loosen my grip on the knife.

Taking a deep breath in, I relax my body into

Dean's. Holding my head up higher, I will not let some tall blonde solicitor intimidate me. Dean is marrying me tonight. I have no reason to feel insecure.

"Hey, babe?" I direct to Dean, while staring at Stephanie.

"Yeah, Princess?"

"How inconvenient would it be for us to find a new solicitor tomorrow?" I ask with a smile on my face.

Bray laughs a little too loudly next to me. I elbow him in the ribs to shut him up.

"Oh, hunny, you're new here. So, I will forgive you for not knowing how things work around here. You don't pay my fees, sweetie. You can't fire me." She picks some imaginary fluff off her dress.

I see that Josh is getting out of his seat across from me. He's seated right next to where she's standing. I kick him under the table, the movement stopping him from getting up.

"Oh, I'm sorry — I didn't know. Who is it, exactly, that pays your fees?" I ask her.

"That would be McKinley Industries." Stephanie smirks.

"Oh, so you'd need to be fired by, I don't know, what do they call that person that runs the big companies? Oh, yeah, the CEO. You can only be fired by the CEO of McKinley Industries?" I ask her, using the ditsiest voice I can muster. Dean chokes on his drink, his grip now firmly around my waist — like he's afraid I'm going to get up and wipe the smile off his solicitor's face.

"That's right, hunny. Now, should we get on with this? I have other meetings to be at tonight. Dean, I know you said you didn't want a prenup, but really, someone in your position needs one. I drew an iron-clad one up today."

"Hold on a sec." I hold my hand up to stop her annoying voice from carrying on. Looking at Josh, it's hard to believe he's the CEO of a billion-dollar company. He's covered in tattoos and piercings—not your average nine-to-five look at all.

"Joshy," I say, giving him my sweetest voice.

"Yes, sweetheart." He smirks. He's smart. I can tell. He knows what I'm about to ask him.

"If your new sister wanted one thing as a wedding present, would you give it to her?"

"Anything you want, El. I'll make sure you get it." He smiles.

Everyone at the table is silent, waiting for my request, barring the kids clattering away at whatever they can get their hands on.

"Would you fire your solicitor and get a new one?" I ask.

Josh looks to Stephanie. She stares at him, mouth opening and closing like she doesn't know what to say.

"Check your phone, Miss Stewart. I believe you'll find a message from Daddy," Josh instructs.

She does just that. She pulls her phone out and

taps a few times. Then her face goes beet red with anger.

"Josh, you can't do this to me. You can't be serious. Because of her." She points at me while yelling. She doesn't stop there; no, she keeps yelling. "You will regret this, you stupid skank! You think…" Her words are cut off by the tattooed hand currently wrapped around her throat.

"You know, it appears I don't like it very much when people yell at my sister. Let me walk you out, Stephanie. I think you need some air." Josh lets go of her throat and takes hold of her arm. Stephanie's whole body begins to shake. She's pale.

"No, it… it's okay. I can find my own way out," she stammers.

"I insist." Josh starts dragging her out of the room.

"Joshua, I'm sure her father is expecting her home in one piece," Dean yells out to their retreating backs.

"He's not actually going to do anything to her, is he?" I ask Dean.

"Ella, Josh can be a little unhinged at times. It's best not to encourage him," Dean says.

"A little is an understatement. Ella, that guy makes the Joker look normal," Bray tells me.

"Well, maybe, but he's been nothing but pleasant to me." I shrug. Who am I to judge? I have enough crazy problems of my own.

"Don't you think it's a little odd, how protective he seems of you? Dean, that's odd, right? He's a legit psychopath. He doesn't care about anyone," Zac interjects his thoughts.

"That's not true; he loves his pigs," Dean says seriously. "Plus, what's not to love about Ella? It would be strange if he didn't like her."

"Okay, whatever. How are we going to do this now if we don't have a solicitor?" I ask.

"I can witness it. Go on, sign your lives away." Josh waltzes back into the room.

I pick up the pen. "Where do I sign?" I ask, looking at the paper.

"Here. Oh, wait, I'm meant to ask if anyone objects to this union? But if you do, you might want to reconsider your objection. For your own health and safety." Josh looks around the room.

"Okay, sign here, Ella. Dean, you sign here." Once we've both signed, Josh takes the paper, signs and then hands it to Zac.

"We need one more witness," he says, handing Zac the pen.

Zac signs the paper then hands it back. "Congratulations, you're married. You can kiss the bride etc. etc." Josh waves his hands around.

Dean grabs my face between his hands and slams his lips onto mine. The kiss is just getting heated, and I'm about to crawl into his lap, when I hear a loud throat clear. That's when I remember we are not alone.

Breaking away from the kiss, I stare into Dean's eyes. So much love and emotion stare back at me. "I can't believe we're actually married. It is real, right?"

"As real as it gets, Princess." Dean picks my hand up, digs into his pocket and pulls out a rose gold ring. It's flat with little pink diamonds all the way around it. It's also very familiar. This is my mother's ring. How the hell did he get my mother's ring? Tears fall down my face as he removes the ring he gave me only hours ago. Once he has the band on, he slides the engagement ring back into place.

"I don't have a ring for you. Fuck, why didn't I think of that?"

"Does she cry like this a lot?" I hear Josh ask Zac.

"Unfortunately," Zac says.

"Does it get any easier? The need to strangle whoever it is that made her cry?"

"Nope."

"Well, we're all fucked then," Josh says.

"Okay, I'm about to remove these headphones, which means you all need to stop the swears," Alyssa scolds.

"Is she serious?" Josh asks me.

"Yep, no swearing around the kid who can talk. Those two can't repeat anything yet, so they don't count," I say, pointing to the twins.

"Aunty El! Aunty El!" Ash starts yelling as soon as his attention is off his iPad.

"What's up, Ash?"

"You bootiful, Aunty El."

"Thanks, Ash. I just got married," I tell him.

"What that?"

"Well, Uncle Dean is now my husband." I have no idea how to explain this to a three and a half year old.

"Oh. Will I get a husband?" Ash asks.

"Only if you want one. You might want a wife," I tell him. He seems happy with that answer and goes back to looking at his iPad.

Dinner was served shortly after we signed the papers. After eating as much as I possibly could of the chicken pesto pasta, I'm now in a food coma. I can't move. I'm so full.

"What's the plan now? When are you heading out to the farm?" Josh asks Dean.

"Tonight. You'll be following, right?"

"Yeah, I got some shit to do. Send me a text and let me know when you're leaving." Josh stands up. "Ella, welcome to the family, Sis." With that, he walks out of the room.

"Ah, Dean, what farm are you going to?" Surely, he's not planning to go away when we just got married. He wouldn't do that.

"*We*, babe. *We're* going out to McKinley Ranch for a few days."

"Dean, we just came back from a few days away. We can't go on another trip. I have to work," I protest. As much as I haven't been looking forward to going into the club, especially now that we don't know where Sarah is, I was still planning on showing up for work tomorrow.

"Ella, you're going to be working remotely for a

while. You can do it from the farm." Zac uses his *dad* voice on me.

"There's stuff I need in my office, Zac. How am I meant to have time to get it?"

"Oh, where's the farm at?" Alyssa asks.

"Down in the Hunter Valley. Why?" Dean answers.

"I think Sarah's planning on going through that way on her way to Tamworth. Isn't that where she said she was heading, Rye?" Alyssa looks at Reilly.

Reilly taps through her phone. "Ah, yeah, she's gallivanting. At the moment, she's in the Blue Mountains, then on Wednesday, they're driving to Tamworth to meet this new boyfriend's parents."

"I'll ask Sarah to bring you whatever files you need, Ella. You should go and enjoy a couple more days away from this slave driver. You just got married." Alyssa's smile is kind.

I don't know how to answer her. How do I tell her I don't want Sarah anywhere near me? Dean beats me to it.

"That'd be great, Alyssa. I've just sent you through the address; send it through to Sarah for us. Come on, babe, we need to pack a few things before we leave."

"Sure." I don't know what else to say. I walk around the table, hugging and kissing everyone goodbye. I thank them all for being here tonight. Regardless of what anyone else thinks, this was my perfect night. I'm married to the man I've always loved.

Chapter Twenty-Four

Dean

"SO, do you want to tell me the real reason why we're going to this farm of yours?" Ella asks.

She's currently sitting in the passenger seat, her legs crossed. We're about an hour into a four-hour drive. My fingers tap on the steering wheel. I can't lie to her, but I really don't want to tell her the truth either.

"I'm hoping Sarah's crazy enough to show up at the farm. Because then we can put a stop to all of this bullshit."

"Do you really think she will? She knows that I know. Why would she show up anywhere I am?"

"At the moment, she thinks you haven't told anyone. The fact that Alyssa and Zac are still talking to her like they don't know anything—that will give her confidence that you're the only one who knows.

For her to continue to get away with this, she wants to silence you before you can tell anyone."

My blood boils at the thought of someone wanting to harm Ella. Glancing in the rear-view mirror, I see Josh's car directly behind me, and then his fucking entourage behind him. We're travelling in a convoy. It's over the top. I wasn't going to take any chances with Ella's safety though.

"Why are there so many cars following us, Dean? It's only Sarah, how much can she possibly do?" Ella asks as she looks out of the side mirror.

"The car behind us is Josh. The ones behind him are his security, not ours, babe." It's not really a lie. Those cars *are* Josh's security. Although I know he only has them following tonight because of Ella.

"Why does your brother need all that security?"

I laugh at her question. "Josh is a crazy motherfucker, Princess. He pisses people off on a daily basis. People with endless means. He has enemies worldwide, no doubt."

"Oh, don't you worry about him? I mean, if people are after him, what if something happens to him, Dean?"

I look across and examine her. She's worried about Josh, someone she met only a few hours ago. To say their instant connection is weird would be putting it lightly. "You don't need to worry about him. He can take care of himself."

"Maybe someone ought to worry about him. He is your brother, Dean."

"I know he is, which is why I also know I don't need to worry about him. I know he won't do anything to hurt you, El. I've actually never seen him be protective over anyone or anything other than his damn pigs. Someone could point a gun to my head and he wouldn't bat an eye. But for some reason, he's taken a liking to you. I don't get it."

"You don't get why someone could possibly want to be my friend?" She folds her arms over her chest; my eyes are drawn to her breasts as they get pushed up from her movements.

"That's not at all what I meant, Princess. What I meant was that Josh has never had an actual friend. Ever. Apart from me. He doesn't really like people very much so he tends to steer clear of them."

"Well, then, that's just more reason why I'm going to be his friend." Her smile lights up her face.

"You are maybe the only person that's ever wanted to be his friend, babe."

"That can't be true. I bet he has women falling at his feet and wanting to be his friend." Ella laughs.

"Well, good genes run in the family." I smirk at her. "There was one girl in high school, who tried to befriend him. She learnt her lesson really quick that Josh was not someone that wanted friends. Poor girl, she never stood a chance."

"What happened to her?" Ella's eyebrows draw down in concern for someone she doesn't even know.

"Babe, as much as I love how kind your heart is and that you want to be friends with my brother, it's our wedding night. I'd prefer not to be talking about Josh."

"I like being married to you," Ella says around a yawn.

"I fucking love being married to you, Princess. Go to sleep. I'll wake you when we get there." Picking her hand up, I kiss each one of her knuckles before resting our entwined hands on my thigh again.

"I'm not that tired. I'd rather keep you company," Ella protests. Five minutes later, she's out of it.

It's dark by the time I pull into the farm. Stopping directly in front of the doors to the house, I jump out of the car at the same time Josh pulls in behind me. Ella is still asleep in the car. I stop at the back of the car, where I can see her through the windows still.

"Is she good?" Josh asks me. I'm thrown a little by his question. I don't think I've ever heard him ask about how anyone else is.

"She's good." I nod. "What are you up to, Josh? What's the deal with Ella?" I ask him

"I'm not up to anything. She's your wife, in case

you forgot during the whole five hours you've been married," he grumbles.

"Seven hours. But that's not the point. Why do you seem to care so much? It's fucking weirding me out."

"You and me both, brother. I don't know. It's not like I fucking want to. I don't know what this feeling is. Something in me tells me she needs to be protected. I don't want her to get hurt." His face scrunches up; he looks pained. "You know, it's almost like that with you. You're my brother, so I don't want to see you hurt. And I would rain hell down on anyone who thought they could harm you. I just happen to like her more than I do you." He shrugs.

"Yeah, I get it. That girl is my whole world, Josh. Nothing can happen to her."

"Don't worry, I got this. As soon as that fucking bitch shows up here, I'll make sure she never breathes the same air as Ella again."

"Okay, let's get inside. It's late," I say as I head to the passenger side and pick Ella up out of the car.

She stirs in my arms. "Are we there yet?" Her eyes slowly open.

"Yeah, Princess, we're here." I kiss the top of her forehead.

Ella's head pops up and looks around. She spots Josh standing in front of the door, holding it open.

"Hey, Josh, you and I are having breakfast together. Meet me in the kitchen at seven thirty in the morning," Ella informs Josh of her plans. He's a little unsure how to respond to her. It's amusing really, watching him squirm.

"Why?" he eventually asks her.

"Because you are my only friend here, and I like having breakfast with my friends," she says. I'd like to know why I'm not included on her list of friends. I should be at the fucking top of the list.

"Babe, I'm pretty sure I'm at the top of your friends list." I know I sound like a wounded child. I just don't care.

"Well, yeah, you're my only friend who gets to see me naked. But I am having breakfast with Josh."

I look to Josh, who still doesn't have any idea how to handle the situation. He eventually agrees to meet Ella in the kitchen before stomping inside.

I take Ella straight to the bedroom I've always used whenever I come back here, which is not very often. The last time I was here was over a year ago— for my father's funeral. It was not a sad occasion, and he's certainly not missed by anyone.

Sitting her down on the bed, I walk over and pull a shirt out of the closet for her to sleep in. As much as I'd love to have my way with her right now, I know she's tired.

"Here, you can sleep in this if you want." I hand her the shirt. Ella puts the shirt on the bed as she stands and starts removing her clothes, her eyes never leaving mine.

She tugs her singlet over the top of her head, then slowly unbuttons her jeans and drags them down her legs. When she stands back up, her fingers trail up her smooth stomach before reaching around and unclasping her bra. Letting the white lace fall to the floor, she's now standing in front of me in nothing but a little piece of matching white lace covering her pussy.

Fuck me, she's fucking beautiful. I'm staring, my eyes taking in every inch of her curves. She then removes her panties, the last bit of fabric she had on. Turning around, she pulls back the covers and climbs in the bed.

"Are you coming to bed?" Her voice is husky with need. I don't need to be asked twice. I strip out of my clothes, and by the time I make it around to the other side of the bed, I'm slipping between the sheets naked.

The moment my back hits the mattress, Ella is on top of me. Straddling me, she positions herself above me. Wrapping one hand around my cock, she strokes it up and down a few times before she lines the tip up with her entrance.

My hands go to her hips, fingers digging into her flesh as she slowly, torturously, sinks herself onto my cock. We both moan once she has fully sunk down, her wet, warm pussy wrapped around my cock like a fucking glove.

Ella starts rocking her hips back and forward slowly. "Princess, I don't know how long I can take this kind of torture," I say through gritted teeth.

Ella pauses her movements. She worries her

bottom lip between her teeth. "Am I... Is this not good for you?" she asks.

"It feels fucking amazing. You feel fucking amazing, Ella. The sight of you on top of me, your tits bouncing around as you grind your pussy on me... The feel of your tight, wet pussy strangling my cock... It feels too fucking good — that's why I'm about to come after thirty seconds, like a fucking fifteen-year-old."

"Oh, well, do you want me to stop?" She smiles down at me.

"Fuck no, you're not stopping. You started this. Now you gotta finish it, babe." I start to rock her hips back and forward, guiding her movements.

"Oh, fuck, Dean! I think I like this position best." Ella groans as I lift my hips, pushing my cock as far in as I possibly can. I'm not going to last much longer like this. I need to get her off first. I need to feel her come around my cock.

I release my hands from her hips, one landing with a hard sting on her ass. I fucking love how responsive she is, her harsh intake of breath, the way her pussy just got instantly wetter. I snake my other hand up to her throat, squeezing a little, as I bring her face closer to mine, causing her clit to rub against my pubic bone.

Her whole body shakes and convulses as she comes undone, her juices leaking all over me and her screams echoing through the room. Just seconds after her pussy chokes the life out of my cock, I'm filling her up with my seed. Pump after pump, it feels like I come for hours.

Letting go of her throat, I watch as her body slumps down on top of mine. My fingers trail up and down her spine as we catch our breath.

"Dean, I really like sex with you," Ella's sleepy voice whispers.

"That's probably a good thing, considering I'm the only person you're ever going to have sex with." I laugh as I kiss the top of her head. "I love you, Ella. Always have. Always will."

"I love you too. Thank you for marrying me." She yawns.

"Trust me, babe, I'm the one winning out with this marriage of ours. I'm batting way out of my league here."

"No, you're not. But can we talk about this in the morning? I'm really bloody tired."

"Sure, babe. In the morning. Go to sleep."

Chapter Twenty-Five

Ella

I WAKE with the warm sun on my face. I slide out from under Dean's heavy arm. It's a more difficult task than one would think. He wraps that arm around me like a damn vice. It's almost like he's afraid I'm going to disappear.

I write a quick note for him and leave it on my pillow — like I have every day this week.

Dean,
Gone to the kitchen for coffee and breakfast with Josh.
Xoxo
Ella.

Every day, since I've been here, I've met Josh for breakfast. He's slowly warming up to me more and more each day, and slowly letting me see glimpses of himself that I doubt anyone else gets to see. To say Josh is complicated would be putting it lightly.

Dean and Josh have both been hovering over me all week. It's like they're expecting the boogeyman to show up and jump out of the shadows. Sarah's obviously not going to show up here. She would have done that by now if she was planning to.

Alyssa called a few days ago to apologise. She said Sarah had changed her plans and wasn't able to drop the files off that I wanted from the club. I ended the conversation as quickly as I could. How could I pretend like everything was okay? Like her best friend wasn't stealing from her? The only reason why I'm not telling her is because as long as she doesn't know, she is probably safe.

I'm up earlier than usual today. Josh won't be down in the kitchen until seven thirty. I have half an hour before he gets down here. This is probably my one chance to go and explore outside a little before everyone else gets up. I throw on a pair of wellies and a cardi that I left hanging by the back door and head towards the horse stables.

Over the last week, Dean's been teaching me how to ride. To say I'm a beginner would be an understatement. I do love the animals though, one in particular, Pixie. She's white with brown socks on her feet. Her mane is a beautiful chestnut colour. I could spend hours brushing and talking to her.

I head over to Pixie's stable. I probably should have brought an apple out for her.

"Hey, beautiful girl." I stroke her nose as she sniffs at my chest over the door. There's a commotion a few stalls down. One of the larger horses starts bucking around and making loud noises.

"What's wrong with him? Not a morning horse?" I ask Pixie, laughing at my own joke. Just as I turn to go and check out what's causing him distress, something hard hits my head.

I can feel myself falling; my vision blurs as I hit the ground. I can make out a blurry figure leaning over me before darkness takes over.

"Argh." Why do I hurt so badly? My head feels like a thousand elephants are stomping around in it. Reaching my hand up to the side of my head, I feel wet stickiness. Bringing my hand back down, I see that my fingers are now covered in blood. What the hell happened?

I remember talking to Pixie, then nothing. Looking around, it's obvious I'm not in the stables anymore. The room is dark; a putrid, damp smell fills the air. I'm sitting on an old mattress, in the corner of a room. I can see a sink along one wall. And that's it.

The room is barren. There are two windows along one wall with metal bars across them, letting in slithers of sunlight.

Dragging myself across the floor, I pull myself up, using the window ledge to help balance me. I'm dizzy. My head is aching and spinning. I feel nauseous.

Stopping my movements, I take a few deep breaths in with my eyes closed. Focus, Ella. You have to focus and get out of here. Walking slowly along the wall, I find a door; it would have been too easy for it to be unlocked. I spend more time and energy trying to budge the handle than I should have.

Slumping down next to the door, I need to rest for a bit. I just need to close my eyes for a little longer. Then I'll have the energy to get out of here. I'll be able to break the glass... call out for help... something.

I come to again when the door handle jingles, opening and closing quickly.

"Good, you're awake. You and I need to have us a little chat." Sarah sneers at me as she leans down into my face. She's resting a small pistol on her leg.

"I have nothing to say to you."

"Oh, but I have plenty to say to you, little Ella. You've ruined everything for me. It was all working out fine until you had to come home." Sarah stands and starts pacing around the room.

"You stole from your best friend. You stole from my family. Why? You know Alyssa and Zac would have helped you if you needed help."

"You don't get it. No one gets it. That should be me. I should be the one living the life of luxury, not a care in the world. I was the one who pushed Alyssa to go out that night. I should have gone myself. Then Zac would have seen me. He would have saved me."

I watch as Sarah taps the gun repeatedly on her thigh, while she walks up and down the small room. This bitch is crazier than I thought. I don't know how I'm going to get out of this situation. I know I need to keep her talking, but the more shit that comes out of her mouth, the crazier she's sounding. And the angrier I'm getting.

Getting angry right now won't help. I need to focus. I need to calm my rapid heart. I absently scratch at my wrist as I take deep breaths. I want to close my eyes and focus on the pain. The pain in my head. The scratching on my skin. I want to let the pain take over and soothe me.

I can't close my eyes though. I can't take my eyes off her. I need to be prepared. Sarah stops moving and stares at me. She looks directly at my wrist, which is now bleeding from my own nails digging into it.

She lets out a cackle. "I know what you're doing. I've heard all about your little mental health issue." Pulling out a tie from her back pocket, she walks towards me.

"You're not escaping that easy, bitch. Hold your arms up, wrists together." Sarah tucks the gun into the waist of her jeans. She yanks on my arms, holding them together. I should fight her. I should try to overpower her, but as she pulls me around, the room starts to spin again. I know I don't have the strength to overpower her yet.

"What exactly is your plan here, Sarah?" I ask as she ties my wrists together. I use the trick Bray taught me, the one where I place my wrists in a position that makes it look like the ties are tight. I'll be able to get my hands out of this when I have more strength.

Sarah slaps me across the face. "I don't have to answer to you, cunt. You are nothing. Do you think anyone is going to miss you? They're not. I bet no one even knows you're missing yet. We're going to wait until dark. Then I'll be able to get out of here without detection. I'm smarter than you, Ella."

She drags me across the floor, away from the door. I can see the small bits of sunlight through the window. That's all I can see though. I can't see any buildings, trees, nothing. I have no idea where we are. We must still be on the farm.

"Do you really think you'll make it off this farm without Dean finding you?" I ask. My heart aches when I think about what he must be going through looking for me. Oh god, what if he called my brothers? They'd both be on their way here.

I feel like hours pass. I've tried to keep her talking as much as I can. Sarah sits across from me with the gun pointing directly at me. She's been rambling about how it should have been her with the easy life instead of Alyssa. That she was prettier. That she was more suited to be with someone like Zac.

I have no idea what happened to the Sarah I met four years ago. This clearly isn't her. She needs serious help. A white jacket, meds, a padded room—the whole works.

I see a shadow move outside the window above Sarah's head. I send a prayer up to whoever listens that someone has found me. My heart sinks when I see a girl pressing her face into the window. She sees me. I see the moment she notices me. Her big blue eyes widen in shock. I give a slight shake of my head; she cannot come in here.

From where she's standing, she can't see Sarah. "No!" I yell out. She ducks her head down, under the window.

"Sarah, you can't do this. What do you think Dean and Josh will do when they find you? I can help you. Let me help you!" I yell as loud as I can, trying to relay to the girl to go and find Dean or Josh. To tell them where I am.

I don't know how long I've been in here. My whole body aches. My head is still pounding. My own yelling is making me feel nauseous.

"Nobody is going to know. Did you think they'd be out looking for you? Where was Dean for the four years you were gone? Huh? Did he ever come to visit you? No." She shakes her head at me, then smirks.

"Do you know why? I'll tell you. Because he was too busy fucking every chick who walked into the club. I even warmed his bed more than once. But I won't bore you with the details of how he likes to choke his women while he fucks them."

My blood boils. She's wrong. She's just trying to get in my head. I know that, but it does not stop the tears from forming in my eyes. How does she know about the choking if she doesn't have first-hand knowledge?

I'm being irrational. Dean was not the virgin. *I was.* Of course he's slept with other women. But Sarah. Really? Why did he have to sleep with her? My fists clench. I want to choke her. I want to watch as that smirk is wiped off her face.

As I'm clenching my fists, the huge rock that Dean put on my finger just days ago digs into my hand. "You know, he may have fucked you. But he married me. Did you hear I'm now Mrs. Dean McKinley?" I smile at her.

It's obvious she doesn't know. Her eyes widen in shock before she quickly smooths out her features. "Well, it's going to be a short-lived union. Don't worry, I'll be sure to keep Dean company while he's a grieving widower."

I'm about to tell her to get fucked when the door's kicked in, the action causing us both to jump and scream. Sarah drops the gun in her shock, and the gun, which I thought probably wasn't even loaded, goes off. As it turns out, it was loaded. Very loaded.

Chapter Twenty-Six

Dean

EIGHT HOURS earlier

When I walk into the kitchen, I'm expecting to be greeted by Ella's voice as she chatters away to Josh over breakfast. Every day this week, she has made a point to meet him for breakfast. I'm not sure he does too much talking during these meetups. That hasn't deterred her though — she's made up her mind they are friends, whether he wants to be or not.

Josh is sitting at the counter drinking coffee. *By himself.* Looking around the kitchen, I note that Ella is nowhere in sight.

"Where's Ella?" I ask Josh.

He shrugs his shoulders. "Haven't seen her yet. Thought she was still in bed with you."

It's ten past eight. She should have been here forty

minutes ago. "She left her usual note, saying she was coming down here to see you. Where the fuck is she?"

Josh stands up, heading for the doors. "She probably went out to see the animals or something. Come on. She couldn't have gone too far."

I barge past him and start yelling out her name as soon as I get outside. It's irrational. I know. But something in my gut is telling me something's wrong. Please don't let that be the case.

"Ella!" I scream as loud as I can. The dogs start barking.

"Ella!" Josh joins in on calling out to her. "You go over to the equestrian yard. I'll head to the stables." Josh starts running towards the stables.

Something is wrong. She wouldn't wander off for this long. I run around the other side of the house, calling out her name as I go.

Fuck, she's not anywhere in sight here either. I make my way back around, towards the stables. Josh comes screaming towards me on a dirt bike.

"Go get a bike and start scouring the fucking farm!" he yells at me over the revs of the engine.

"What'd you find in the stables?"

"There was blood on the ground out front of Pixie's door. Drag marks leading out the back of the barn. Dean, we're going to fucking find her. Get your shit together and get on a fucking bike." He takes off towards the far paddocks.

I call Zac on my way to the shed.

"Yeah?" he answers.

"Zac, you gotta get down here. Ella's missing." As much as I'm trying to keep the panic out of my tone, it's not working.

"What do you mean she's fucking missing? Where the fuck is my sister, Dean?" he yells. I can hear Alyssa in the background, telling him to calm down.

"I don't know. She's been getting up early and meeting Josh for breakfast. She didn't show up to meet him this morning. Just get here, man."

"I swear to God, Dean, if your psychotic brother has done something to her, I'm gonna kill him."

"It's not Josh. You haven't seen them together. He's different with her."

"I'm on my way. Fuck. I'll get Bray and we'll be there soon."

The phone cuts out. I jump on a bike and start making my way through the tracks towards the front of the farm.

An hour after hanging up, Zac and Bray are landing on one of the paddocks in a fucking chopper.

"Anything?" Zac asks as he storms towards me. If ever there was a time that I thought my best friend would off me, it was now.

"Nothing."

"She couldn't have just fucking disappeared into thin air. We just have to keep looking. We will find her." When it was that Bray became the voice of reason, I do not fucking know.

"Yeah. Josh has three chopper crews about to start searching from the air. We have every man and his dog out searching through the bushes and tracks, all over the farm. I've put guards on the gates. No one is getting off this farm." I lead them towards the equipment shed.

"Grab a bike and let's go." I have to get back out there and keep looking. I have to fucking find her. She's my everything. Without her, I have nothing.

It's been hours. She's not anywhere. I've scoured every damn inch of this farm. She has to still be here somewhere. There's only one way in and out that leads to a road. No one has gone out that gate all day. I've checked the footage of the cameras all around the buildings.

We saw Ella walk towards the stables around 7 a.m. And then nothing. It's like she's fucking vanished. We also saw footage of Sarah sneaking around the stables not long before Ella went in.

"How certain are you that she hasn't been taken off the farm?" Bray asks from the deck. He's been staring out at the empty fields, like Ella's just suddenly going to appear there.

"There's only one way a vehicle can get in and

out. She's still here somewhere. We just have to find her. We will find her," I grit through my teeth.

I have to find her. Because the alternative is not one I can contemplate. Josh has had three choppers in the air for hours now, searching all the bushland on the outskirts of the farm. They just keep going around and around.

Every member of staff on this fucking farm is scouring the acres of land looking for her. Some on foot, others on horses or quad bikes. Yet, there's still not a fucking clue where she could be. When I do find her, I'm putting a goddamn tracker on her ass.

I once thought Zac was a fucking idiot for putting a tracker on his fiancée. Now, I wish I'd have fucking thought of doing that.

"We know Sarah can't just drag her off the farm without a vehicle," I rationalise, not sure if I'm trying to remind myself, or the others that she is still here somewhere.

"I'm going to fucking kill the bitch. Motherfucker!" Zac throws the glass he was holding.

No one says anything. We are all feeling the exact same way. Whichever one of us finds her first will take pleasure in erasing Sarah from the world.

"I'm going to go watch the footage again. Make sure we haven't missed anything." I slam every door in my path on the way to the office.

Hours have passed. It's late afternoon. I can't fathom her being out there scared, and in the hands of a fucking psycho, for this fucking long. What if I can't find her before dark? I know Ella is strong. But how much can one woman take?

Josh walks into the office, shutting the door behind him. I've never seen him so rattled before. The fact that he is even the slightest bit worried, *that* is fucking me up. He's never been worried about anything or anyone.

"Why do I feel like I'm a fucking volcano about to erupt and spill blood everywhere?" he asks.

I look him over. His body is tight, his hands opening and closing into fists and his jaw ticking.

"You're angry, Josh. That's what it feels like to feel something for someone else," I tell him.

"I don't fucking like it. I was content not caring. Why the fuck did she have to go and make me fucking care?"

"She's not the first girl to make you care. She's just the first you can't scare away. We will find her."

"The pigs are starving. The sooner we find this Sarah chick, the sooner they'll be able to eat." He smirks. And we're back to my psychopathic brother. This Josh, I can handle. I know what to expect.

The angry Josh, who's unpredictable and frankly, scary as fucking shit. "We're going to find her. I have to. I only just got her back. I can't lose her, man. I just can't." My eyes water with unshed tears.

"I'm going to go back out. Check down near the river again," Josh says. As he turns the handle of the door, his phone rings and his whole body goes stiff.

He pulls his phone out of his pocket, staring at the screen while letting it ring.

"Who is it?" I ask?

"It's Emmy." He doesn't look like he's going to answer. I press the green button and bring the call up on speaker phone. His voice cracks as he answers the call.

"Emmy, what's wrong?" Josh asks after a moment.

"Josh, I… I'm down at the cabin. Um… our cabin. There's a girl in there. She's in trouble, Josh. I saw through the window. I went to help her, but then she started yelling at someone named Sarah. And she… she said your name. I don't know what to do… What do I do?" Emily's voice cracks over the phone.

"Where are you now?" Josh asks as he storms outside and jumps on a quad bike. I'm hot on his trail. I have no idea what cabin Emily's talking about. But I have no doubt my brother knows exactly where it is.

I signal for Zac and Bray to follow. They do so without question.

"Stay hidden, Em. Do not come out of that spot until you hear me or Dean calling for you, okay?"

I don't hear her reply before he cuts the phone off and starts heading towards the scrub behind the stables.

We ride for twenty minutes before we come to a stop behind Josh.

"We need to walk from here. About five minutes away, down that direction, is an old cabin. Sarah has Ella holed up in there. The cabin only has one door and two windows. Let's go," Josh says as he leads the way.

When we come to a small clearing, the cabin comes into sight. Bray starts running towards the door before we can come up with any sort of organised plan. Well, fuck, I guess this is how it's happening.

That fucker is fast; he has the door kicked in before any of us make it there. As soon as he disappears through the door, a gun goes off.

"Ella!" I scream as I barge my way through the door, almost tripping over Bray, who is now squirming around on the fucking ground. Ella's sitting against the wall, dried blood down the side of her face.

I lean down in front of her, gently cupping her face in my hands. "Princess..." There are so many things that I want to say to her right now. I want to yell at her for leaving the house alone. I want to tell her how much I fucking love her. I want to cradle her in my arms and never let go.

"What took you so long?" she asks with tears falling freely down her face.

"You are never leaving my side again! I mean it. I will handcuff our wrists together if I have to." I gently lay kisses all over her face.

"Where are you hurt?" I ask as I start to loosen the tie holding her wrists together. She manages to twist her hands around, pulling them free before I get the knot untied.

Her eyes go wide as she looks at something behind me. Then I hear it. That snap. That very unique sound of a neck being snapped. Ella gasps as she covers her mouth with her hands.

A brief look over my shoulder confirms my suspicions. Josh is standing above a lifeless Sarah. With a smirk on his face, he tells Zac, "I'll be back to clean this mess up later. Don't fucking touch it."

He's about to walk out of the cabin, when he turns back and walks over to where Ella is still sitting on the floor in front of me. Josh reaches a hand out, brushing her hair out of her face. I expect Ella to flinch away from his touch after what she just saw. She doesn't even bat an eyelash.

"I'm really fucking glad you're okay, sweetheart," Josh says, kissing her forehead.

"Thank you. I'm really glad you're okay too," she tells him.

Josh steps over Bray as he walks out the door.

"It's okay, fuckers. I'm still alive down here. Don't worry about me. I'll just bleed out quietly."

"I wish you'd fucking bleed out quietly, idiot," Zac says.

"Hey, I don't see your ass on the ground with a bullet in it. Why the fuck am I always the one who has to get shot?"

Zac bends down to inspect the ass that just got shot. "Because you're reckless. You deserved that, barging in without a second thought. Also, the bullet only fucking grazed your ass. Grow a pair and harden the fuck up," Zac grunts out.

"I want to go home," Ella whispers to me.

"Let's go." I pick her up and carry her out of the building. I sit her on the front of the quad bike, just as Josh comes around from the back of the house, carrying a screaming Emily over his shoulder.

"Put me down, you asshole! I can bloody well walk, you know!" she yells at him while hitting on his back. Josh continues on without saying a word. He places her on the dirt bike, jumps on behind her and kicks the bike to start. Within seconds, they're out of sight.

"Who's the blonde?" Ella asks. "Is she going to be okay?"

"She'll be fine. Josh, not so much."

"Who is she?"

"She is Josh's undoing—Emily."

Epilogue

DEAN

TWO YEARS later

I'm sitting on the deck of our beach house, watching Ella float around in the waves. I've been watching for a while now, but she's only just noticed that I'm up.

She still has a habit of getting up early and leaving the fucking bed without waking me. I swear I'm starting to get grey hairs from the stress of waking up and her not being there. Even after two years, my first thought every morning is her. When she's not in the bed, I panic. She doesn't know this of course.

A mixture of thoughts of her being taken by someone, or her hurting herself, runs through my head every fucking morning. I can't shake the feeling that something bad will happen if I take my eyes off her for too long. She is better though. We found a new psychologist in Sydney for her. She has gone sixteen months without cutting.

She tells me the need to cut isn't there anymore. I can tell there are times she thinks about it though, the way she digs her fingers into her palms. She looks around the room searching for something. The way she silently counts to ten taking deep breaths, I know she fights these demons still. I'm right here beside her, fighting them with her.

That panic in the mornings never soothes until my eyes land on her. The beach is the first place I look. Nine times out of ten, she's swimming. I don't know where she keeps finding those pathetic bikinis though. I've destroyed every pair I see on her. Yet, every damn morning, she's sporting new skimpy two-piece swimmers.

This morning is no different. I groan, my cock hardening at the sight of her walking up the beach towards me, her long, dark, wet hair falling over her shoulders. She's wearing a bright pink string bikini, her golden skin shimmering as water drips down all over her.

My eyes roam from her face down, my cock hardening more and more, the further down her body my eyes travel. I can't help the smile that comes at the sight of her little round belly. At four months pregnant, Ella has never been more beautiful.

She's a fucking goddess. One that I thank God for every damn day. Her tits bounce in the tiny bits of fabric as she picks up her pace, climbing up the steps to the deck.

"Morning, you're up early," she says as she bends

and twists her hair around, wringing water from the locks.

"You weren't in bed." I shrug in response.

"I felt like a swim. I didn't want to disturb you," Ella says as she comes over and straddles me. Her arms go around my neck, her wet body pressing up against me.

My hands grope at her ass, her full, soft cheeks fill my palms. "Mmm, I like it when you disturb me," I mumble into her neck as I lick the salty water from her skin.

Ella grinds her pussy into my cock. Ever since getting pregnant, she's horny twenty-four seven. I'm not about to ever say no to her. "I can disturb you now."

"Oh yeah? How you gonna do that?" I ask her. Leaning her body back, I move the fabric of her bikini top away, take one of her nipples into my mouth and bite down on it.

"Argh, Dean, I need you to get your damn cock out and put it in me now!" She groans as I move on to the other nipple. Her impatient hands dig into my boxers, pulling out my cock. Her hand fists around me, stroking up and down.

Pulling on the little strings on the side of her hips, I watch as the material falls away, revealing that pretty fucking pussy I can't get enough of. Ella lifts her hips and sinks herself down on my cock in one go.

"Fuck, I love how your pussy wraps around me,

Princess. So. Fucking. Wet. So. Fucking. Tight." I grunt out between thrusts.

Before long, we're both heading over the edge.

"Dean, I'm going to…" She doesn't finish her sentence, her words turning into sounds of pure pleasure, as her orgasm hits her. Her juices soaking my cock while her pussy convulses around me sends me over the edge with her.

I hold her close as we both catch our breath. "I know that you're not a spring chicken anymore, but do you think we can do that again? Or do you need a few hours?" Ella giggles at her own joke.

"Babe, really? I'm about to show you just how young I still fucking am." Carrying her into the bedroom, I lay her out on the bed. "I fucking love you, Ella McKinley. Always have. Always will."

"I love you too, Dean, even if you are getting grey hairs." Her giggles continue to fill the room.

Epilogue

ELLA

SIX MONTHS later

"I FUCKING HATE YOU!" I scream as I throw the plastic cup, completely missing him.

"Princess, I think you need to calm down," Dean says.

"Calm down? You can't be serious? Calm down? You try having something the size of a watermelon come out of your vagina and see how calm you fucking are!" I continue screaming.

"I should have shot you when I had the chance," Zac mumbles, glaring at Dean.

"Hey, El, want me to hit him good for you? Give him a little pain for you?" Bray asks.

I glare at both of my idiot brothers. "Neither of you are touching him! I'm sorry, Dean. I love you, I really do." I'm now crying, tears streaming down my face.

Dean brushes the sweaty hair off my forehead. "Princess, I love you. If I could do this for you, I would."

I brace myself through another agonising contraction. "Oh really? Well, you should! This is all your fault, Dean. You did this to me!" I'm back to the yelling. The smirk that crosses Dean's face at my words does not help my anger.

"Hey, Zac?" I turn my head to look at my brother. Zac stops pacing up and down the small room.

"Yeah, El?"

"I know I said I didn't want you to... but how do you feel about killing your best friend? Because if you don't, I just might." My whole stomach stiffens, and I scream as another contraction tears through me.

"For you, El, I'd kill just about anyone. How bout you let me know tomorrow? If you still want him gone in the morning, it's a done deal." He smiles at me.

"Thanks, mate. What happened to our twenty years of fucking friendship?" Dean questions him.

Zac shrugs. "You slept with my sister."

It's the same response whenever Dean and Zac argue over anything. Zac always comes back to the "you slept with my sister" remark. They're still very much best friends. If you looked up the definition of a Bromance, I'd be surprised if you didn't see their pictures.

"Yeah, I did. A lot!" Dean laughs.

"Well, maybe if you didn't, we wouldn't be in this predicament right now," Bray grunts out.

"Okay, Mrs. McKinley, let's check how things are doing." The doctor walks into the room. Looking up from the chart, she stares at the three men in the room. Asking me, she says, "Which one of these gentlemen do you want to keep around? Because the other two have to go."

Bray and Zac both start to argue, to which, the doctor holds her hand up stopping them.

I make a point of looking between the three, like I am actually going to choose someone other than Dean.

"Princess, I swear to God, don't even think about it," Dean threatens.

I laugh a little. "Those two are my overbearing brothers. They can wait outside."

"Okay, you heard the woman — *out*." The doctor shoos them out the door and shuts it behind them.

"Okay, let's see how far along you're dilated, shall we?"

As she sits on a stool at the end of the bed, positioning my legs up and spread wide, Dean grunts beside me. He has hated every single physical exam the doctor has performed during this pregnancy.

"It hurts so much, Dean. Make it stop," I beg him, even though I know he can't do a damn thing. It's been hours. I've been in labor for what feels like an eternity.

"Ella, one more push, a really big one. Come on, you can do this," the doctor says from between my legs.

I shake my head no. I can't do this. I just want to go to sleep. I just want it to be over.

"Princess, let's just try one more. Okay, you're doing great. Come on, babe, you're Ella fucking McKinley! You can do anything," Dean whispers into the side of my head.

"Okay." I brace myself.

"Ready? One, two, three and push. That's it. Keep going. We're nearly there," the doctor calls out like a damn cheerleader.

I keep pushing, screaming unsavory things as I grit my teeth. Then I feel it happen. The moment the baby is out, I hear the sound of a newborn's cry.

"Congratulations, you have a beautiful baby boy!"

The doctor places my son on my chest. I can't explain the overwhelming feeling of love that washes over me.

DO you want to read all about Dean's mysterious psychotic brother Josh? His story begins in Ruining Her, available now! Continue reading for a sneak peak of Josh and Emmy.

Acknowledgments

I am thankful first to you, the reader, the one whom this story was written for. And I hope that you enjoyed the characters and the emotional rollercoaster that is Dean and Ella's relationship.

Dean and Ella's story took me on an emotional rollercoaster. I cried, laughed and cursed them all in the same day. Their story truly touched my heart. I loved being able to delve deeper into Ella's relationships with her brothers and their wives.

I am thankful to my family. My wonderful husband: whose support and endless encouragement never fails. Nate, I could not have accomplished this without you.

I want to thank my beta readers, Natasha and Amy, you girls are one of a kind. I am forever humbled that you once took a chance on this little unknown author from Australia and stuck around for book one, two and now three. Thank you for all of the time and effort you put into reading and providing insightful feedback for Entwined With Him.

The Kylie Kent Street Team, what can I say? I would literally be nowhere if it weren't for you. I often get asked by other authors how I managed to form my street team. My answer is always the same, one hundred percent pure luck, and I'm not ever giving them back!! I believe I have the BEST street team in the business. Not only do you all ARC read for me, but you all read, promote and share whatever I put in front of you so enthusiastically and with genuine interest and excitement. I freaking love you guys!

I want to thank the guy with the abs on the cover, Jon Collins. I found him on TikTok (where the best cover models are!) You may know him as the onesie king! Jon's positivity and enthusiasm kept me wanting to write, even on days I didn't feel like writing—and there were plenty of those days. When real life decided to throw its curveballs and interfere with my fantasy world that is The Merge Series, I would simply jump on TikTok and watch Jon's livestreams and videos.

He never failed to make me laugh in his many onesie costumes. His videos reflecting on never giving up, even when you have no fight left inside of you—of not judging others—truly impacted the way I wrote Ella's mental health journey and the way her family helped her. Jon's messages touch millions of people; he uses his influence to help those in need and spreads positivity, laughter and kindness in all of his livestream sessions. I am honoured to have been able to collaborate with him for the cover of Entwined With Him.

About the Author

About Kylie Kent

Kylie made the leap from kindergarten teacher to romance author, living out her dream to deliver sexy, always and forever romances. She loves a happily ever after story with tons of built-in steam.

She currently resides in Sydney, Australia and when she is not dreaming up the latest romance, she can be found spending time with her three children and her husband of twenty years, her very own real life instant-love.

Kylie loves to hear from her readers; you can reach her at: author.kylie.kent@gmail.com

Let's stay in touch, come and hang out in my readers group on Facebook, and follow me on instagram.